BIONIC BUTTER

A THREE-PAWED K-9 HERO

RADA JONES

Illustrated by
MARIAN JOSTEN

APOLODOR

This book is a work of fiction. Names, characters, places, and incidents are the product of the author's imagination or are used fictitiously. Any resemblance to actual events, locales, or persons, living or dead, is entirely coincidental.

Copyright © 2021 by Rada Jones

All rights reserved.

No part of this book may be reproduced in any form or by any electronic or mechanical means, including information storage and retrieval systems, without written permission from the author, except for the use of brief quotations in a book review.

APOLODOR PUBLISHING

ABOUT THIS BOOK

Dear reader, Butter and I are glad you're here.

This K-9 memoir is a work of fiction. Dogs don't write much, and they publish even less. They can read into our souls, but their spelling is nothing to write home about.

That's why I wrote Butter's story. Over the years, I've belonged to many dogs who taught me to love and talk Dog, then abandoned me for the rainbow bridge. As Butter says, speaking dog is kind of magic. It's not about how you roll your tongue to make silly sounds. It's about watching, smelling, and feeling each other into your hearts. That's why dogs don't lie. How can you lie when you taste someone's tears, lean against their thigh and listen to their heartbeat? There's no room for deception in Dog like there is in human language.

Butter is a mellow yellow Lab who loves food and hates fights. She'd take a brownie over a brawl any day of the week, but sometimes you have to fight, whether you like it or not. That's how K-9

Butter, AKA Three-Pawed, became Bionic Butter, a hero who changed peoples' lives.

This book is a love letter to Butter and all the other dogs who make our world a better place.

Rada

ALSO BY RADA JONES

BECOMING K-9: A Bomb Dog's Memoir
(K-9 Heroes Book 1)
ASIN: B08XKBGXN3

K-9 VIPER: The Veteran's Story
(K-9 Heroes Book 3)
ASIN: B095N21LSD

OVERDOSE: AN ER PSYCHOLOGICAL THRILLER
(ER Crimes: The Steele Files Book 1)
ASIN: B07K1FGN6D

MERCY: AN ER THRILLER
(ER Crimes: The Steele Files Book 2)
ASIN: B07VYVPFFF

POISON: AN ER THRILLER
(ER Crimes: The Steele Files Book 3)
ASIN: B07YYLSQ8L

ER CRIMES: The Steele Files Books 1-3
ASIN: B08BTY9LSC

STAY AWAY FROM MY ER, and Other Fun Bits of Wisdom
Wobbling Between Humor and Heartbreak
ASIN: B083TYXVVG

Dedication

To dogs:

May you spend forever with your loved ones. You deserve it.

To humans:

May you become the person your dog thinks you are.

EPIGRAPH

"*Dogs do speak, but only to those who know how to listen.*"

Orhan Pamuk

BIONIC BUTTER

1

The lamb aroma hits my nose with a vengeance. I open one eye to see Brown stirring the magic lumps into my kibble and dousing them with boiling water and the scent makes me drool.

I lick my lips and wag my tail in appreciation.

"It's lamb! Guys, we got lamb."

I love lamb! It's my favorite, right there with beef, chicken, and fish. Especially the way my mom cooks it. She stuffs it with cloves of garlic, then rubs it with Dijon, rosemary, and thyme. And salt and pepper, of course. She cooks it on high heat, so it stays pink inside. But Diane is half a world away while we're at our base in Kandahar. And this isn't real lamb; it's the MRE, Meals Ready to Eat, version of it, and it stinks. But it still beats plain kibble.

"The heck lamb, that is ancient mutton, *quoi*," Viper growls, his French accent still thick with sleep. "I bet it died of old age. They must smell it from Helmand."

He crawls out of his crate and shakes, and just like that, he's ready for the day. His head held high, his sharp ears up, he wrinkles his dark nose at the fake lamb aroma. Viper's not a foodie. He'll turn up his nose at kibble, but give him a ball, and he'll work all day. But he has some redeeming features. Like he lets me finish his meals. I'm so grateful I'll even put up with his obnoxious Belgian Malinois attitude.

"Helmand? You've got to be kidding. They've got to smell it all the way back home."

Guinness crawls out of her crate to practice her morning yoga. She lifts her black snout in the air in an upward dog, then rears her rear in a downward dog, then shakes like she's been crawling through mud, and she's good for the day.

No wonder. Guinness looks slim in her sleek black coat. And she's young. She's only three and a German shepherd, while I'm six, and a bit on the chubby side. But that's just because I'm a yellow Lab. I bet I'd look thinner in black.

I'm still younger than Viper. He's got to be as old as the hills. He was here when I arrived for my first deployment, years ago, and I bet he'll still be here when I'm gone, since Viper lives for his job. Detecting explosives is all he knows and all he wants to know. Out of us all, K-9s and humans, he's the only one glad to be here. Everyone else can't wait to go home.

No wonder. With the humans' cots at one end and our crates at the other, this hangar is nobody's idea of home. It smells like BO, boots and gun cleaner, and other things that shall not be named. The soldiers plastered the plywood walls with pictures of their kids and dogs and green places where it sometimes rains, but that doesn't make it home. Oh well. At least we're safe here, inside the wire. And there's food.

"You guys are too picky. You'd complain if they fed you hot fries with ketchup."

I turn my tail to them and taste my food. The scent is potent, the taste not so much. It could use some garlic, real lamb, and a better chef than Brown.

Guinness sighs.

"I could go for some fries, especially if they came with a cheeseburger." She picks up a piece of kibble, sniffs it like she's looking for IEDs, then drops it to the side.

Viper shakes his head.

"Fries are nothing but salt and fat. You guys need to make better choices if you want to stay in shape."

He turns his pointed black nose away from his food and makes a show of cleaning his privates, like either Guinness or I give a poop. But that's Viper. He's an athlete, and he gets his highs from working out. He's one of those nuts you see on YouTube standing on top of a hydrant, jumping over a six-foot fence, or walking a tightrope. That's why he's nothing but muscle, iron will, and green bile.

Guinness ignores him like she usually does.

"Have you guys heard the plan for the day?"

"More of the same, I bet. We take our handlers for their walk, train them to look for explosives inside the wire, then dinner. Boring," Viper says.

"You don't think we'll go outside the wire?"

"I wish we would, but we've been out every day this week. The humans may need some time to recover."

"I do too," I say, licking my bowl clean. "I need my beauty sleep."

"You certainly do." Viper snickers, then leaps aside when I pretend to jump at his throat.

"You're wrong, Viper. There's no rest for the weary today," Guinness says, as Silver, her handler, slips her bulletproof vest over her head and buckles her in.

"Like really? What's wrong with these people, eh? Can't they take a day off?" I growl, eyeing Viper's bowl.

Viper nuzzles the bowl toward me.

"The insurgents must have different priorities."

Brown brings my bulletproof vest, slips me a cheese cracker, and rubs my ears with his large brown hands. He's my handler, and I've known him since I could fit in the palm of his hand. Six years later, he's still my favorite human other than Diane.

"It's our turn in the lead today, Butter. Are you ready?"

"Almost."

I grab a mouthful from Viper's food as Brown buckles my vest. I'm glad we're in front. When you're in the back, you swallow everyone else's dust, and you have no choice but to follow. In the lead, you breathe the cleanest air and get to set the pace. There's always a chance that you'll step on a mine and blow up, eh, but I'm not worried. I'm no longer a rookie; this is my fourth deployment, and I know how to take my time. Better slow than dead, Brown says, and I agree.

"Your turn again?" Viper mumbles as Sabrina kits him up like the rest of us. He's in the middle today, and he hates it. He'd rather lead, of course. We all do. Not today, Malligator.

The lieutenant, a short guy with sun-fried skin, briefs us.

"Today's mission is searching for explosives in the village compound. The insurgents stepped up their game. Almost every day, we find new IEDs. They must have explosives hidden somewhere. We need to find and destroy them. Brown and Butter, you're leading today. Good luck."

We file out in the yard. The massive green gate creaks open, and I step out. Brown follows, thirty feet behind me on his leash, to be safe in case I step on a mine. The others are even further back. Guinness and Silver come last.

I stop to take in the terrain. Tan dust covering the scorched earth as far as I can see. Nothing moves but a plume of smoke rising over the village, bruising the pale-blue sky. A few tortured bushes bake under the merciless sun. It's so hot that I'm grateful for the dust protecting my paws from the heat, as much as I hate breathing it.

Somewhere far behind, Viper barks.

"Do not rush, Butter, *ma chère*. After all, we have nothing better to do than watch the dust all day."

"Shut up, Viper. She knows what she's doing better than you do."

That's Guinness, of course. But Viper's right. There's a limit to how long we can stand this heat, we K-9s in our fur coats and the humans in their heavy armor and equipment. I step forward, trying to ignore the dust filling my nose as I sniff for IEDs. But this dust is so light it's everywhere. There's no fighting it, no avoiding it, no ignoring it. The one thing I can do is accept it and focus on the only thing that matters: keeping us all alive.

`

2

I get moving. Step after careful step, I sniff my way along the half-mile dusty path to the village. The others follow me far behind. I don't find much other than the dust: motor oil leaked from a truck, a cigarette butt, somebody's spent chewing gum, the spot where Viper peed yesterday.

Even more than the heat and the dust, the silence gets to you. There are no birds, no cars, no wind, no laughing children. Nothing but the soldiers' footsteps muffled by the dust and the occasional metal clanging against metal as they stumble under their heavy equipment.

We're all hot and tired when we reach the compound, but there's no time to rest. We divide into teams to check the dozen tiny homes. They aren't anything like American homes, with their basements, garages, sheds, and tons of stuff. These are just mud huts with curtains instead of doors and no furniture to speak of, but for a chest, a rug, and maybe a water jug. People here have even less than we have at our base. Our humans have cots, tables, and chairs, while we have our crates. These people have little more than what they wear. And they are not like our soldiers.

Males cover their faces with fur, while females cover their hair with veils. They wear loose fluttering clothes to keep them cool. They're loose enough to hide suicide vests, so we, K-9s, have to sniff them close and personal to keep our humans safe.

The first hut is empty. There are two men and a kid in the next one, who watch me with wary eyes as I sniff every jug, every pot, and the painted chest in the corner. Brown waits outside to be safe if I blow up.

I find nothing, so I move on to the people, even though they aren't friendly. I sniff their robes, their feet, and their hands as they watch me with hard eyes. They all smell like anger and fear. I don't think they like me. Not even the kid who stares at me like I stare at cats: I ache to grab and shake them, but I know better.

I step out and wag my tail to tell Brown that I'm done.

"Nothing here."

We join the others. They didn't find anything either, so we file back into formation to head inside the wire. That's what we call our camp since the ten-foot mud wall that surrounds it is topped with rolls and rolls of razor wire to keep out the uninvited. It's not pretty, and it won't give you the warm fuzzies, but it keeps us safe.

We head back the same way: Me first, dragging Brown behind me, then the others. I sniff carefully every time I take a step, even though I just did it an hour ago. Why? You never know. What if some joker planted an IED when we weren't watching, hoping to get us on our way back? Because that's what they do.

I reach the end of the compound wall, and I'm about to step out in the open when I get a whiff of something funky. It's somewhere to my left, behind the wall. I lift my nose to catch the wind, but the dust makes me sneeze.

"Hey, Butter! No rush, *ma chère*. You do not want to mess up your pretty blonde tail."

Viper, of course. I turn around to tell the ice-hole where to put it when the earth explodes under my feet.

3

It's not the earth that exploded. It's me.

A wave of pain rips through my body like a blasting grenade. I try to think, but the pain garbles my thoughts and scorches my brain. I'm nothing but a mass of pain.

Where am I? Who am I?

I hear someone scream, and it turns out it's me. I strain to breathe, but the dust clogs my throat and I shrivel as the burning pain squeezes the life out of me. Then the taste of dust reminds me.

I'm Corporal K-9 Butter, serving in Kandahar. I was on patrol, and I'm hurt. Did I step on an IED? Wouldn't that be stupid!

Brown kneels next to me and runs his hands all over my body, looking for injuries. I know he's careful, but everything hurts so bad that I cry.

Brown sniffs.

"I'm sorry, Butter. We'll take care of you."

He touches my leg. The pain explodes in me like an IED, and I scream again.

"Butter! How are you, Butter?"

That's Guinness, far away. I hear the panic in her voice, and I try to answer, but I can't. I'm too weak. I yell as the men lift me on a stretcher.

"Good luck, Butter, *chérie*" Viper barks as he leaves with Sabrina and a few men. "We are going to find the bandits who hurt you, and we will bring them to justice. I will see you at the base."

I smell Guinness coming, and she tries to stop by, but Silver won't let her.

"No time, Guinness. We need to rush Butter to the base where we can take care of her. Her life depends on how fast you can get her inside the wire."

Guinness runs to take the lead, and we get moving. The soldiers carry me on the stretcher as Brown holds my paw. A new stab of pain pierces my leg every time the men take a step, and they move so fast it feels like they're running, but they can't be. Guinness must sniff her every step; she can't go that fast. But she does.

Another burst of pain clouds my brain, and my world goes dark.

I wake up inside the wire. Brown holds pressure on my paw while Silver sticks a needle in my other leg and hangs a bag of fluid. Guinness squeezes between them to lick my nose. Her amber eyes are worried, and I know she's having an awful day even though I can't lift my head to sniff her butt.

"How're you doing, Butter?"

"I'm OK. Thanks for taking over and bringing us back to the base."

"Don't mention it. You're doing great. You'll be as good as new in no time."

I sigh. As sick as I am, I can still smell a lie. But it's coming from kindness, so I let it go.

"Thanks, Guinness. I need to close my eyes now."

I lay in a fog. Whatever Silver gave me dulled the pain but muddled my brain even more. I'm too tired to open my eyes; I'm too tired to think; I'm too tired to live.

I hear them fussing around me. Brown tightens the tourniquet around my wounded leg while Silver gives me another shot. Someone calls for a helicopter; then the gate creaks open. The patrol is back.

I smell Viper. At least I think it's Viper, though he's never smelled like this before. He smells worried, anxious, and afraid, but that can't be. Viper doesn't know how to be afraid.

"How is she?"

Guinness growls.

"I don't know. They called the helicopter. It should be here any moment."

The helicopter rumbles closer and closer until it's so loud it covers everything else. The dust fills my nose as it lands, and I sneeze.

I feel the stretcher moving under me.

"Bye, Butter. I love you."

That's Guinness. I choke, and I don't know if it's because of the dust or because of Guinness's love.

"Love you too."

"Come back soon, Butter. I will save my lamb for you."

That's Viper. That promise is as close to mentioning love as I ever heard from him.

Then it gets dark.

4

I don't remember who I am, but I see myself free-falling through a tunnel of swirling rainbows. I spin faster and faster, and the colors blend around me, pulling me in. I claw the air to slow down, but I find nothing to grasp on to. There's nothing here but the rainbows sucking me in. My stomach fills my throat, and I'm about to get sick when a voice breaks through the ringing in my ears.

"It's OK, Butter. You'll feel better soon. We'll take care of you."

I don't know who that is, and I'm too dizzy to open my eyes. I sniff a human female smelling like deodorant, disinfectant, and blood.

A hand pets my head, another one holds my shoulder. That anchors me enough to slow down the rainbows until they become the ordinary colors of ordinary things. A white ceiling, dark green walls, a gray concrete floor, a young female in blue scrubs petting my head. She bends over to wipe my muzzle with a wet cloth, and I smell Cheetos on her breath. My stomach twists, and I want to puke, but I drool instead.

"There now. See? You're better already."

I don't think so, lady. I'm dizzy, I'm sick to my stomach, and everything hurts, especially my left front paw. I'm lying down, but that darn paw feels like I'm walking on hot coals. I twist to reach over and lick it, but I can't. It turns out that I'm tied down. Where the heck am I? And how did I get here?

I cry for help.

"Guinness? Viper? Where are you?"

My throat is so parched that my tongue sticks to the roof of my mouth, and I can barely whimper.

"There now. Just a few more minutes to make sure you're OK; then I'll take you to your crate to take a nap."

"Where's Guinness? Where's Brown?"

"There's a good girl. You want some water?"

"I want Guinness. Where is she?"

The human brings a water bowl. I lap a little to wet my throat, but I'm so weak I have to lie back.

"See? Isn't that better already?"

"No. Where's Guinness?"

She pats my head.

"Good girl."

I'm so muddled it takes me a moment to figure out whether she's deaf or stupid. It turns out she's neither; she just doesn't speak Dog. Some humans do; some don't. Some are born with it. Some learn it as they live with dogs. Some never do. Most humans who work with dogs speak the language; otherwise, they couldn't function. Brown does, like all the handlers. But most of the soldiers, no matter how nice they are, don't get it. Speaking dog is kind of magic. It's not about rolling your tongue and making silly sounds. It's about watching, smelling, and feeling each other into your hearts. That's why dogs can't lie. How can you lie when you taste someone's tears, lean against their thigh, and listen to their heartbeat? There's no room for deception in dog like there is in human language.

But what's this girl doing here if she can't speak dog? Fortunately, I don't have much time to ponder.

"How's she doing?"

A pair of camo pants blocks my view. They contain a male smelling like iodine, soap, and stale coffee. He bends over to listen to my chest and push on my belly, and I'm about to upchuck on his silly paper booties when he steps back.

"She's doing great, Doc. She just had some water. I'm about to take her to the kennel."

"There's no hurry. Why don't we keep an eye on her a little longer, just to make sure she's OK? She's been through some rough times, and she's not quite out of the woods yet. Are you, girl?"

He leans over to shine a light into my eyes, then opens my lips to peek inside my mouth. His tired eyes are blood-red, and he's got fur around his mouth, unlike any human soldier I ever met.

"Where am I?"

"You're in the veterinary hospital. You got shot on a mission. Your bullet proof vest saved your life, but your paw didn't fare well. It must hurt."

It does.

"You've just had surgery. We worked for hours trying to save your paw, and it's still a little touch-and-go. We'll have to watch it closely for another day or two before we know where we stand."

I don't get what he says, and I don't care. But at least I can talk to him.

"Where are my people?"

"Your handler just went to get some rest, but I bet he'll be back tomorrow."

"Where's Guinness?"

"Where's what?"

"Guinness. My best friend."

He sighs.

"He must be in Afghanistan. You're in the best veterinary hospital in the USA, getting the best care a K-9 can get. But now you need to sleep; otherwise, you can't heal. Why don't I give you something to help you relax?"

He pushes something from a syringe into the tube in my leg. My pain dulls, then vanishes, and I get lighter and lighter, like a feather, until I melt into the sky.

5

The kennel smells sick. Dozens of dogs, some big, some small, some purebreds, some mutts, all reeking of pain and worry as they struggle to unwrap their bandages and shake off their cones of shame. And most of them are K-9s.

How do I know? By the smell. K-9s come in all sizes, shapes, and colors, but we all live for the job. We can smell that on each other like humans can smell perfume.

"How ya doing, girl?"

I struggle to lift my head. A white pit bull with one black eye sniffs at me across from my cell, wagging his hot-dog tail like crazy. He looks just like the dog in the Target commercial, and he grins from his black ear to the white one, despite his cone of shame and the bandages around his leg and chest.

I wag my tail—sort of.

"Fair to middling. You?"

"I'm good, thanks. So good to meet you! I can't wait for breakfast."

His short tail quivers with excitement as he dances on his feet, even the one that's in a cast. He's the happiest K-9 I've ever seen, so much so that I start to wonder if he is a K-9 at all. We, K-9s, are all sorts of wonderful, but happy is not at the top of the list.

He points his nose toward me and sniffs until the dust from the floor makes him sneeze. I know he'd love to get properly introduced and smell my butt, but we're too far apart.

"What's your name, lovely lady?"

"Butter. I'm K-9 Corporal Butter. You?"

"I'm Target."

No kidding.

"Are you a K-9?"

"Of course. I am a qualified customs agricultural agent. I work for the TSA, where I sniff for smuggled agrarian products. Say somebody tries to smuggle in lemons from Sicily or oranges from Costa Rica. Unless properly inspected, they may bring in diseases or aphids that could destroy our crops. My job is to find them and stop them. I also sniff for contraband animals. My sister Raisin works in the field too, but she specializes in Coconut Rhinoceros Beetle Larvae. They are the bane of palm trees."

"Wow. I didn't know such a job existed."

"Sure, it does. It's essential, and also lots of fun. I once found a suitcase full of pangolins."

"Penguins?"

"Not even close. Penguins are those fat birds dressed in tuxedoes. Pangolins are small animals wearing scaly armored vests instead of fur. They look funny, like miniature dinosaurs, but they're useful since they eat ants and termites. Sadly, Chinese traditional medicine practitioners believe their scales and meat have healing properties, so they pay big money to get them. Poachers bring them over from Sri Lanka and the Philippines. They pack them like oiled sardines, so most of them don't make it through the trip."

"That's terrible."

"Yes. Especially if you're a pangolin."

I try to imagine being locked in a suitcase with a dozen other dogs, but I can't. Good. I'm already miserable enough. Fortunately, the whole kennel starts barking, so I forget what I was worried about.

"What's going on?"

"They're bringing breakfast."

Breakfast! I try to stand, but my left front paw wants none of it, and I fall on my side as my leg explodes with pain.

Target cocks his blocky head, his nose wrinkled in worry.

"Are you OK?"

"Middling. You?"

"What happened to you?"

"I was on a mission. Then I got here."

"How?"

"I don't know. How about you?"

He looks down, his ears flat with embarrassment.

"I... I was stupid."

"What did you do?"

"My handler and I were going home after our shift."

"And?"

"I saw a cat."

"Yes?"

"I... I was a bad dog. I took off after it, and I got hit by a car."

"I'm so sorry, Target. That's terrible!"

"Terribly stupid. But enough about me. What happened to you?"

That's so unusual it makes me wonder if Target is really a male. He smells like one, but he's so caring you'd think he's female. Most males seldom remember to ask you how you're doing, and they never do it twice.

"I don't know."

I try to remember. We went on patrol. We were searching for explosives in the village near our base. I was leading the team inside the wire, then...

"I got shot."

"Where?"

"In Kandahar."

"No. Where in your body?"

"I don't know."

"What hurts?"

"Everything."

"What hurts the most?"

"My front paw."

"Do you still have it?"

What a silly question. Of course, I do. It's right there, bandaged, painful, and useless as it is. I can't stand on it or even lick it, but it's there.

"Sure."

"Good. Because some canines lose it, and that's the end of their K-9 career."

"Really?"

"Yep. Does it hurt?"

"Like a son of a gun."

"That's great. It's bad news if it stops hurting."

"Why?"

"Because it's like with us. When you stop hurting, you're dead."

6

Eating breakfast while lying on your side is not for the weak, I tell you, but one's got to do what one's got to do. I'm a big fan of food—fast food, slow food, cat food, any food. Food is almost as important to me as my people and my job. Even more than my naps. But sadly, this breakfast is nothing to write home about. It's even worse than the MREs in Kandahar. Those at least pretended to smell like something, whether lamb, beef, or chicken, while this here is just a sloppy porridge. But it softens my throat and fills the void in my belly. I always feel better when I eat. Even the pain in my leg starts fading.

Since I'm lying down anyhow, I catch a nap. Technically, since I'm sitting still, I guess you could say that the nap caught me. Either way, my skin gets all prickly, and I wake up. You know, like when somebody stares at you? It's Brown, and he's beat. His uniform looks slept in, his eyes are red, and his mouth has thinned to a line, but his hands are gentle as he pets my ears.

"How're you doing, Butter?"

I slap my tail to the ground.

"Better now that you're here. Can we go?"

I struggle to stand, but I fall on my nose, and Brown's tired face crumples. He sniffs and wipes his eyes with his sleeve.

"Not yet, baby girl. Not yet. You've got to feel better first."

"I feel fine."

He clears his voice.

"I just spoke to Silver. Guinness and Viper send you their best wishes. They all miss you and can't wait to have you back."

I wag my tail. My best friend Guinness, AKA Corporal Guinness Van Jones, is all into combat, apprehension, and that sort of stuff. She's an MPC, Multi-Purpose K-9, just like Viper, but Viper is a Malinois, so we call him the Malligator. We work together on detecting IEDs, but I'm a Labrador and not much into fights. I'd rather eat or nap. We're all different, but they're my brothers in arms, and I miss them terribly.

"Tell them I miss them, eh? I can't wait to be back."

Brown blows his nose.

"Sure. But you need to get better first. Diane called too. She says she misses you. Her cooking hasn't been the same without your help. Aleta and BB send their love."

Diane, my mom, is Brown's wife, and Aleta and BB are my sister and brother, even though neither can sniff bombs or grow a tail. Aleta at least can tell when the bacon's burning and such, but BB can't talk yet, and he can't sniff either. They're my family, and I miss them. I love kids. They are fun to play with, and they always drop food, so I help clean. Some tasks are tastier than others, though. I could do without pumpkin and applesauce, but fries and peaches? Sign me up. As for cookies…

"Aleta started kindergarten. BB is walking now. He's not talking yet, but he should be soon. After all, he's almost three."

"I'm sorry, but the doctor wants to see her now."

It's the same female who doesn't speak dog. Today, she doesn't smell like Cheetos. She smells like bubblegum, and that's even worse. Speak about an evil thing! You chew it within an inch of its life, only to find your teeth glued together. The last time that happened, Brown had to pull my jaws apart to unglue me so I could eat and drink.

Brown picks me up gently and helps me to the stretcher.

"May I come along?"

"I'll ask the vet."

As we head out the door, Target barks.

"Hang in there, Butter. You've got this. You'll be like new in no time."

The door closes before I get to answer, but his words do me good. I can use some encouragement. As much as I love Brown, he acts like he's at a wake. Mine.

7

But we're not going to a wake just yet. We're back in the rainbow room that looks just the same, but for the rainbows. Brown helps the tech move me from the stretcher to a well-lit exam table. The lights above me are so bright that I have to squeeze my eyes shut for fear they will melt my brain.

The doctor is waiting for us, and today he smells fresh like coffee and soap, and his facial fur is gone. He smiles at me and nods to Brown.

"You must be her handler."

"I'm Brown. I trained Butter since she was a pup. She's my partner and my friend."

"Lovely dog."

Brown frowns.

"Butter is more than a dog. She's an explosive detecting K-9 who performed so many successful missions that nobody knows how many lives she saved. Mine, for sure, more than once. Throughout her career, she never made a mistake. And getting shot was not her fault. She's not only a hero, but she's great company. Always patient, happy, and loving."

My heart goes all warm and squishy when I hear Brown talking me up. Brown's a good man, but he's not much into PDA. He'd rather feed me than praise me when I get it right, and that's fine with me. I'll take a cookie over two commendations any time. But right now, I can use a pep talk. I'm a little down on my luck, and between getting shot, leaving my friends, and being locked in this darn kennel, things are getting to me.

The vet comes over to check me out. He pets my head and scratches me behind the ears.

"Butter, you're a lucky girl to have such a loyal friend in your handler. Let's check your paw and see how your luck holds."

He holds up my paw, and the tech starts unwrapping the bandage. I brace for pain, but I can barely feel them touching me. Yesterday's agony has dulled into numbness, so much so that I can't even feel it when the vet pinches my toe.

"Does it hurt?"

"No."

He picks up a large needle and sticks it in my toe. I see it go in, but I feel nothing. It's like it's someone else's paw.

"How about this? Does this hurt?"

"No."

You'd think he'd be pleased, but no. His face darkens as he mumbles something to himself, then puts on a pair of thick lighted glasses that make him look like a giant bug. He touches, pulls, and prods every inch of my paw. Boy, am I glad it no longer hurts! He brings it to his nose and sniffs it like I've never seen a human do. He's got good technique, too, four short sniffs in, one out, then repeat. I'm impressed! But why my paw and not my butt?

I'm just about to ask him when he shoots his blue rubber gloves in the garbage, then turns around to speak to Brown.

"This is no good."

Brown stares at him like he's lost it.

"What do you mean it's no good? Didn't you hear her say that it didn't hurt?"

"Exactly. Sticking needles in your toes should hurt. If it doesn't, that means the nerves are dead. I did my best to repair the ruptured blood vessels, but it doesn't look like it worked. There's not enough blood getting to her paw to keep it alive. And if the nerves are dead, I'm afraid the paw is dying too."

The paw? Dead? My paw? But I'm alive. How can my foot be dead?

Brown measures him with narrowed eyes.

"So what are you going to do about it?"

The vet sighs.

"I'm afraid we'll need to amputate her foot. Otherwise, the infection will spread through her body and kill her."

Brown's hands close into tight fists, and his head juts forward like he's about to punch the vet. He's got a short fuse, Brown, and his size alone is enough to scare most people. But the vet doesn't blink. His clear blue eyes look past Brown's rage into his soul.

"Wouldn't you rather have her live?"

Brown's anger melts. His shoulders drop as he shrinks into a sick shadow of himself. His eyes look everywhere but into mine, and he sighs.

"If you have to..."

Are you freaking kidding me? My blood boils, and I see red.

"Hey, humans! Are you speaking about me? How about speaking to me? What the heck's going on? What are you talking about? What's amputeete?"

The tech blows her nose in a corner, but nobody cares about her. I only have eyes for these two men who talk about me like I'm a defective fire hydrant.

I glare at the doctor and bare my teeth. He rolls his stool toward me and puts his hand on my shoulder.

"I'm sorry, Butter. I'm afraid we'll have to cut off your paw to save your life."

"What? Have you lost your mind, eh?"

That's not polite, I know, but he's got me frazzled. There's only so much that even a meek Canadian like me can take before she blows a gasket.

"Butter, your paw is dead. We need to cut it off; otherwise, it will poison your body, and you'll die too."

"Nonsense. My leg doesn't even hurt anymore."

Then I remember Target. "Legs are like us. When they stop hurting, they die."

Mine stopped hurting.

"What will she do without her leg?" Brown asks.

'She'll have to learn to walk on three limbs. Most dogs do, especially the young ones."

"She's no longer young. She's almost seven."

"And she's a big girl. We may be able to get her a prosthesis."

"Will she go back to work?"

"In Afghanistan? Definitely not. The war is over for her."

Brown wipes his eyes with his sleeve and looks away, and for the first time in my life, I'd love to bite him if I could.

"Are you crazy, man? The vet says I can't go back to my job and to Guinness and Viper? And what do you do? You just stand there and say nothing?"

I try to lunge, but I'm strapped to the darn table. So I bare my teeth, growl, and bark up a storm to make sure they get how I feel. Brown looks away.

"I'm sorry, Butter."

The vet plunges a needle in my neck, and it's all rainbows again.

8

The searing pain in my leg rips through the fog in my brain. Where the heck am I? The sharp odors of chlorine, blood, and fear fill my nose, and it all comes back to me. I got shot, and now they want to cut off my paw. Seriously?

I lift my head to see Target's eyes, the white and the black, glued to me.

"Hi, Butter."

"Hi."

"How ya doing?"

I don't know. I shake my head to get rid of the fog, but a stab of pain pierces my leg, and I whimper.

"Sorry, buddy."

"Not your fault."

I glance at my leg, and my heart skips a beat. My paw's gone. Like, gone. Vanished. All that's left of my leg is a stump encased in a stiff white bandage. I stretch to lick it, but the cone of shame won't let me get close. I pant in agony. I didn't know pain like this existed. It's like someone nailed my paw to a board, crushed it, and set it on fire. It hurts so bad I can barely breathe. But how can that be? The paw's gone. So, if it's gone, how can it hurt?

My whole body, from my nose to my toes, throbs with waves of pain. I brace myself to resist it, but that makes it worse. This is more terrible than the day I got shot. Then I didn't know what happened. Now I do, and this knowledge dwarfs the pain in my leg. My working days are over, and I'll never see my friends again. I'm so desperate that I can't help but whine.

Target's little tail quivers, and his whole butt shakes with it in encouragement. He dances on his paws, sending me good vibes, but I'm not in a place I can receive them.

"It's OK, Butter. It will soon get better, you'll see. They'll give you something to make you better in no time."

"How would you know, eh?"

I don't know where that came from, but I'm embarrassed. It's not Target's fault; he's just trying to make me feel better. But I'm too hurt and too desperate to apologize, so I turn my back to him and lie there, panting to soften the ordeal until the tech comes to check on me.

"You're hurting, aren't you? Let me give you something."

She slips me a pill, and the pain starts to fade. So does Target and the kennel, and all of a sudden, I'm no longer in the hospital. I'm back to that other kennel where, a lifetime ago, Brown came looking for a dog.

I was so small that I could barely see and hear, and I was too young to walk, so I crawled. My brothers and sisters snored, piled on top of each other, as I crawled around looking for food. I heard the door creak open like it did whenever we got fed, and I looked up.

Way above me, two humans stood looking, their heads close to the sky. I cranked up my head to see them better, but I lost my balance, and I fell.

The male laughed.

"They're so cute. How old are they?"

"Four weeks."

"Really? How come you got them so young?"

I recognized the female. She always brought the milk.

"It's a sad story. Some puppy-mill owner had his champion Labrador bitch escape. She came back pregnant, but they weren't purebred, so he couldn't charge an arm and a leg for them. He dropped them here instead of letting their mom look after them until they're old enough. In his business, time is money. The longer she has them, the longer it will take her to have another litter. But we were glad he didn't drop them in the dumpster."

"That's terrible."

"It is. You wouldn't believe the things humans do to dogs. We see them all here. You want a male or a female?"

"A male, maybe?"

"These two. The rest are females."

She pushed forward Brown and Black.

The man kneeled to see them, though there wasn't much to see. He petted Brown with one hand and Black with the other, but they didn't care. They burrowed further into the bedding, looking for milk. That's the thing with boys. They're slow. They hadn't figured out there was no milk in the bedding. Milk only came from the humans.

I was hungry, so I headed toward him, wobbling on my shaky legs, and I latched on to his finger.

He laughed.

"This one is something else. What's his name?"

"That one is a girl. She's Yellow."

"Yellow."

He picked me up and held me in his palm. He looked into my eyes and stroke my head. It felt good, so I sighed and settled in.

"Would you like to feed her?"

"Sure."

He fed me a syringe full of milk. I drank it, then the next and the next.

"She's hungry."

"She's always hungry, that one."

I was about to fall asleep in his hand when he stood up and cleared his throat.

"I'll take her."

The door slams, and I wake up to realize that it was just a dream. I'm no longer Yellow, the puppy Brown took home six years ago. That's just an old memory, so old that I never remembered it until now.

Brown adopted me and we trained for months before we deployed to Kandahar, where we went through mission after mission, detecting explosives and saving lives.

We were a team, Brown and I. Darn it, we were more than a team. We were a K-9 unit.

Then I got shot.

I lost my paw, and he abandoned me here.

9

I lay in my cell forever, torn between the wound in my leg and the agony in my soul, until I fell asleep. I woke up thinking it was all just a dream. One of those dreams like when you chase a cat and you're about to catch him, then he turns around, and you find he's a lion. This whole shooting thing must be just a nightmare. I can't wait to wake up and tell Guinness and Viper all about it after I gulp my mutton slop.

But the pain in my paw is real. The whimpering of sick dogs and the smell of disinfectant drag me back to reality and I open my eyes to Brown staring at me, his cheeks wet with tears.

"Hi, Butter."

He sits next to me on the floor and pets me through the kennel grates. That makes me so sad that I want to weep, even though dogs don't cry. Not even when our humans do.

"How are you?"

"I'm OK," I lie.

"Good."

We sit next to each other, the silence between us a chasm neither of us wants to cross. Brown clears his voice.

"The doctor said they had to amputate."

I say nothing.

"But he says you'll get better soon. The pain will go away, and you'll be able to eat and drink as usual."

For the first time in my life, the thought of food leaves me cold. There are things in one's life more important than food. Not many, mind you, but there are a few.

"Then what?"

Brown sighs.

"The doctor said they'll try to get you a prosthesis."

"What's that?"

"That's like a boot made to support your leg so you can walk again."

"What if they don't?"

Brown bites his lip and looks away, and I feel sorry. He's trying to make me feel better, and I'm not helping. But I can't. What will I do if I can't walk? How will I search for IEDs if I can't run and jump? How will I play with Guinness?

The enormity of my loss crushes me. I lay my nose to the ground and close my eyes. I don't want to make Brown feel bad, but it's like: Who am I if I'm not an explosive-detecting K-9? What am I here for?

"I don't know, Butter. I wish I did. I'll try to find out."

"OK."

He leaves, and I lie awake thinking. Will he go home? Will he tell Diane and the kids? Will they stop loving me now that I lost my leg and I'm useless? I choke with sorrow, and my heart bleeds as I miss my people. Especially Diane.

I'll never forget the first time I met Diane. The day Brown took me home from the shelter, he put me in the pocket of his jacket. I was warm, cozy, and full of milk, so I fell asleep at the sound of his heart beating, rocked by the rhythm of his steps.

A scream woke me up.

"Really? A puppy? My puppy?"

It was Diane. She picked me up from Brown's pocket and held me to her cheek. Her skin was warm and soft and smelled like food. Her black curls tickled my nose, and I sneezed. She laughed and kissed Brown.

"Our baby! Look at those lovely eyes and those silky golden ears! We'll call her Butter."

Brown taught her how to feed me, and I slept by their bed in a shoebox padded with Diane's old sweater, breathing her scent. Whenever I cried, she picked me up and fed me. I was loved, cared for, and happy.

Then they got Aleta. I don't know where they found her, but she was tiny and soft and smelled like milk. I got to be a big sister, look after her and teach her the ropes. Speak about a hard job! She's beautiful, but boy, was she slow! She took months to start crawling, and I'm still waiting for her tail to grow. But I love her anyhow.

By then, Brown and I had started training, and we spent our days in a vast hangar covered with cans. Some smelled like explosives: TNT, plastics, fertilizer, sulfur; others held all sorts of odors, from food to cats. I sniffed one can after another until I got them right every single time. Whenever I sat by the right can, Brown gave me one of Diane's chicken rosemary cookies.

In the evenings, I played with Aleta. I taught her how to sniff while Diane cooked us cinnamon chili and tiramisu.

The day Brown and I got deployed to Afghanistan, leaving Diane and Aleta behind, was the worst day of my life.

The grief of leaving them tore me apart. Who will look after Aleta? Who'll watch over her and lick her tears? Who'll teach her how to grow a tail?

Diane is a good mom, but she's only human. How will she cope on her own?

"Take good care of Aleta while I'm gone. Don't let her tumble down the stairs. Make sure she doesn't chew on Brown's shoes. You know how he gets."

"Sure thing. I'll look after her, and I'll send you pictures. But promise me you'll look after Brown."
"I will. I'll bring him back."
I did.
But who'll look after him now?

10

I'm not bragging if I say I'm a good napper. I'm the best napper I ever met, in fact. If anyone organized napping championships, I bet you a bowl of kibble against a three-mile run that I would win it no contest.

But sleep wouldn't come near me that night. It wasn't only the pain—the pill helped with that—but I was bewildered. The whole night I struggled to figure out how can I be a K-9 without my paw. And, if I'm not a K-9, then who am I? And what am I here for?

I must have fallen asleep by the morning since I wake up to Target wagging not only his tail but his whole butt to greet me. For a moment, I wonder what his blood tastes like. But it's not his fault, of course. He's just a happy dog, and nothing will change his cheerful disposition.

"How are you doing, Butter? You look lovely today."

I swallow my first two remarks, then my third.

"I'm good. How about you?"

"Excellent. It's going to be a great day. We'll get breakfast, and then we can chat, and then we'll have dinner. It doesn't get much better than this."

"Shut up, Target, you dumb pit bull."

The lugubrious voice comes from a dark corner. It's not loud, just a low, haunting howl, almost too soft to hear, but Target's happy grin melts like a snowman in the sun. He flattens his ears and shrivels, and I feel guilty because that's exactly what I wanted to say. But I didn't.

"Who's that?"

"That's Nora."

I strain my eyes to see her, but all I can see is a shadow. I can't even tell her breed.

"What's wrong with her?"

Target's voice lowers.

"She's dying."

"Why?"

His voice drops to a whisper.

"The old shrew used to be a drug-sniffing K-9 with the TSA. Some folks say she got addicted to drugs, and that's why she got sick. By the time they found out, it was too late to treat her, so she's on hospice care now."

"What's hospice?"

"It's when you're about to die, and they keep you comfortable."

That's an interesting thought. I'd like to be comfortable. But would I want to die?

Breakfast arrives, and it's no better than the last one, but I get it down anyhow. I always feel better when I eat.

"What did you eat in Afghanistan?" Target asks.

"Lamb. Chicken. Beef."

"Wow!"

"Well, not really. It was just kibble, but my handler would add some flavors from a bag, then douse it with hot water, and it wasn't too bad. How about you? What do you eat at home?"

"Just kibble. But then you know what it's like. You pick up after the kids and help clean the dishes, and it's not so bad."

"They never let us clean the dishes. Well, there were no dishes other than our bowls. We only ate MREs."

"What are those?"

"Meals Ready to Eat. It's dried food that comes in a bag. You add hot water, and then it's food again."

"Good?"

"Some better than others. The meatloaf wasn't bad, especially smothered in ketchup, but the Chili and Macaroni Vegetable Lasagna...."

"What do you guys know about food?"

Nora's howl makes Target shrivel.

Not me. There aren't many subjects I consider myself an expert in, but food is my number one. I eat it all, from kibble to baby formula, marrow bones, and chocolate cake. Not at the camp, of course. There was nothing there but MREs. But Diane is a chef with a catering business. She does it all: barbecue, Mexican, Italian, fusion. Whenever she works on a new recipe, she tests it at home first. The kids aren't really into it, but Brown and I help her the best we can. I suggested sprinkling fried okra over her Tacos al Pastor and adding a touch of cinnamon to her smoky chipotle chili. I slobber just thinking about it. I'm an expert, and I won't have some drug-addicted mutt tell me that I don't know my food. So, with a voice sweeter than a well-soaked tiramisu, I ask:

"What sort of food would you like to talk about, Nora? Italian,

Mexican, French? I'm from the south, so I'm partial to barbecue, but we can talk anything from béchamel to sushi if you want."

"Who are you?"

"I'm Corporal K-9 Butter, based in Kandahar, Afghanistan. I've been detecting explosives there for the last five years. How about you?"

The whole kennel holds their breath waiting to see what's going to happen. Chorizo stops chewing on the grates of his cell. Goldilocks forgets he was cleaning his tail. And Target? I think he forgot to breathe.

"I'm Nora."

11

Believe it or not, Nora isn't so bad when you get to really know her. It turns out she's a beagle, like Snoopy, Charlie Brown's famous dog. Her problem isn't her personality; it's her voice. Beagles are adorable. They look like stuffed toys, chunky and spotted, with silky pancake ears falling to their knees. They're cute as heck until they open their mouths. But then, beware! They have this low, haunting howl that makes them sound mournful even when they're having fun, and Nora is no exception.

I meet her in rehab as I struggle to walk on my three legs. And I'm not doing well. I'm good for three steps, but every fourth step, I fall on my face. So I get up and try again. And again.

"Hey, Three-Pawed. Just count to three, and skip the fourth step."

I thought I recognized the low howl from the treadmill, but I couldn't believe that this itsy-bitsy little thing could be the harpy who frightened a pit bull, like Target. I open my mouth to message her the nasties when I see her frail little body shake on her unsteady legs, and I close my mouth. But she persists.

"Seriously. It's like the waltz. 1-2-3, 1-2-3, 1-2-3. Just keep the rhythm and skip the missing paw."

"I don't dance," I growl, but I try to keep the count. 1-2-3, 1-2-3, and for the first time, I don't fall on my face.

"Good job, Three-Pawed."

"My name's Butter, not Three-Pawed."

"And mine's Nora, not Old Shrew."

My ears flatten in embarrassment. I didn't think she heard Target's whispers. It turns out I was wrong.

I go on waltzing as she struggles to keep up with that treadmill that's too slow for a mildly energetic turtle. I start to get the hang of it, and I barely face-plant anymore when all hell breaks loose in the gym. A fancy white poodle breaks a nail and goes into a total meltdown. The therapist rushes to console her as everyone else chuckles.

It feels like an excellent time to waltz toward Nora's treadmill and offer my butt in introduction. She sniffs it politely, then provides me hers. She smells old and sick but not sour, and I wonder what keeps her sparkle going. Once we complete the formalities, we get to chat.

"How does being a K-9 in Afghanistan prepare you to talk about food?" Nora howls.

"Afghanistan surely doesn't. But my mom is a chef."

"A dog? A chef?"

"My human mom, Diane. I never knew my real mom. She worked in a puppy mill."

"A puppy mill!" Nora cocks her head, and one of her pancake ears falls over her face, so she shakes her head to put it back in its place.

"Yes. One of those places that breed litter after litter to make money. They couldn't care less about the dogs."

"I know. I worked in one."

"You? I thought you were a drug sniffer."

"That was my second career. I started as a bitch in a puppy mill, but I stopped being productive when I was five, so my owner dumped me. The human who rescued me worked for the TSA, so I ended up working with him. They didn't care about my puppy production; they only cared about my nose. And nobody has a nose like mine. We, beagles, have the best noses in the world."

I clear my voice, but I swallow my comment. She's not without confidence, Nora, even though she's just a scrawny little thing with ribs sticking out, ears hanging to the ground, and a howl that could wake up the dead. But she grows on you.

"Did you like detecting drugs?"

I bite my tongue, but it's too late. Target said she got addicted; that's why she's sick. What a stupid question! My ears flatten, and I look down in embarrassment, but Nora laughs.

"That stupid Target and his rumors again. That dog doesn't have the common sense of a squirrel crossing the road. Even worse, he couldn't keep his mouth closed if they wired his jaw shut."

I feel bad since Target is my friend.

"Come on, Nora, he's a nice, well-meaning dog."

"He is. He's also a stupid conspiracy theorist. It's not his fault, but boy, I wish he found a grain of common sense somewhere. I don't know if it's those citrus aphids he's been sniffing or if he was born that way. Either way, sniffing drugs didn't get me addicted, just like sniffing explosives didn't make you an insurgent. That's poppycock."

"Why are you sick, then?"

"I got breast cancer because of all those litters I had—eight in four years. And every single damn time, they took away my puppies before they were ready because they wanted me to have another litter. Then another. Every time was another heartbreak. I cried for days, looking for them everywhere. I couldn't believe they were gone. Then I'd have another litter, and I'd burst with joy. I cared for them and loved them, then they took them away again. It's not fun being a bitch in a puppy mill. Don't ever try it, Butter."

Her voice breaks into a heart-wrenching howl that shakes the walls, and every dog in rehab turns to stare at me like I bit her.

"I'm sorry, Nora."

"It's not your fault, girl. How are you doing?"

"I've been better."

"I know. Sorry about your leg."

"Thanks."

"But they make amazing prostheses these days. You may even get to do things you could never do with your own legs. Have you heard about Oscar Pistorius, the Blade Runner?"

"No."

"He's this guy who lost his legs when he was a pup, but he still got to win the Olympics. The other runners wanted him banned. They said that his blades were better than real legs and gave him an advantage."

"Really! Could he jump and sniff explosives?"

"I don't know about jumping, but as for sniffing, I'm pretty sure that's a no. He's human, and with or without legs, they can't smell worth a damn."

Talking to Nora gave me hope. If even a human, as clumsy and slow as they are, could win the Olympics on a prosthesis, maybe I could get one and go back to my work?

12

Life's better in Butterland now that I have friends. Target brightens my mornings with some kind comment about my shiny coat or fluffy tail. I spend endless hours debating with Nora the importance of herbs and spices in Italian cooking before moving on to Mexican or French.

"Absolutely no garlic in fettucine Alfredo! That's blasphemy," Nora howls, and the kennel shivers.

I'm undaunted.

"You'll never know until you try. And you don't even have to mince it; you can just drop a couple of roasted cloves to hint at the aroma."

Nora shakes her head so hard that her ears slap her face. She's a purist and only goes for the classics, while, thanks to Diane, I'm more into fusion.

"That's ridiculous! What are you going to come up with next?"

"Chocolate in chili?"

"No way! Chocolate only goes in mole!"

"Absolutely not! Diane's Chocolate Cinnamon Chili was our best seller. We put it in a bowl of warm sourdough bread and sprinkled it with grated cheddar."

The banter helps us pass the days. It takes Nora's mind off her hospice and mine off my disability and unemployment. Now that my stump is almost healed, I spend day after day in rehab, learning to walk on three legs. But I really look forward to getting my prosthesis. I can't wait until I can run and jump again so I can go back to work. I'm so excited that I bend Target's ear about it every single day.

"With the prosthesis, I'll be better and faster than ever before. Paws are delicate, you know. They get burned when you step on hot metal—and every single freaking piece of metal is hot under the Afghan sun. Paws hurt when you step on sharp debris or thorny branches. The prosthesis will allow me to do things nobody else can."

"But will you know if you step on a mine?" Target asks.

I shake my head, but I keep my patience. It's not his fault he's naïve. After all, he's only an agricultural pit bull. How would he know?

"Prosthesis or not, once you step on an IED, you're history. They're designed to explode at the slightest pressure. Even a freaking cat could set them off. Someone said they trained rats to find IEDs. Rats don't blow up since they're light enough to step on a mine without triggering it. But I think that's poppycock. How would you train a rat to take that kind of responsibility? Rats are unreliable by definition, unlike us, K-9s. Either way, you should never step on an IED. To point them out to your handler, you sit next to them. Touching them is a recipe for disaster."

I lay down to lick my remaining front paw, wondering. Maybe I could get a prosthesis for that one too? From being Three-Pawed, I would become Bionic Butter. I'd love to show Viper and Guinness a thing or two!

"That's wonderful. I can't wait to see your prosthesis."

Target smiles from one ear to the other, his tail going a mile a minute, and his butt follows. He's been a great friend and an excellent companion, always listening and having something nice to say.

He may be the friendliest dog I ever met, no disrespect to Guinness and Viper. They're my friends and heroes, but they're no cheerleaders. They're like: "Get off your assets and get going, will you?" Target is all about: "What a good job you're doing!" I'll miss him terribly when he goes back to his aphids and his pangolins tomorrow.

"I'll miss you, Target."

His wee tail shakes.

"I'll miss you too, Butter. I'd love to meet again. Any chance you'll get to California?"

I hope not. I need to get back to my work and my people, and they're half a world away from California, but I don't want to be rude.

"You never know. How would I find you?"

"The US Border and Customs Protection. Oh, Butter, I'd love to get together if we could."

"Me too, big boy. Me too."

And I'm not lying. When the tech puts a leash on Target to take him away, the whole kennel explodes in loving good-byes.

"Good luck, Target."

"Go get them, orange sniffer."

"There goes the pangolin hero."

Target's butt dances with excitement, and a goofy grin splits his face from his black ear to the white one. Even I sniff a little. After meeting Target, I'll never look at pit bulls the same way. I've heard people calling them cold-blooded mindless killers, but nothing could be further from the truth. There's a big kind heart beating in Target's broad chest. I hope he gets a beautiful life, and he looks both ways before chasing his next cat.

"I'll miss you guys. I hope you all make it home safely."

He's about to step out when a mourning howl makes the kennel shiver.

"Good luck, Target. You need it. You deserve it, too. Just hang off those rumors, will you?"

"Thanks, Nora. Be well."

The kennel feels hollow without him. He was the life of the party, and without him, we're all a little sadder. But it won't be long now. My prosthesis should come any day, and then I'm good to go. I can't wait to show it to Guinness and Viper.

When Brown visits that evening, his eyes are dark with worry, and he smells funny. I sniff again. Sadness, and…guilt? Why guilt? What did he do? He smells just like that time he forgot Diane's birthday. But I'm pretty sure it's not my birthday since I don't have one.

"How're you doing, Butter? What's new?"

"My friend Target went home today. He's going back to sniffing pangolins. I can't wait for my prosthesis to arrive, so I can leave too. I heard they're phenomenal, much better than paws. I'll get to be faster and stronger than I ever was. I'll be Bionic Butter, and I can't wait to show off to Viper and Guinness."

Brown's face melts like snow in the rain.

"What are you saying, Butter?"

Something bugs him, and he's not listening. I start over.

"My prosthesis. With it, I'll be a better K-9 than I ever was. I'll run faster and jump and work better than ever. I can't wait for it to arrive. What do you think? Tomorrow maybe?"

Brown clears his throat.

"Prosthetics are expensive, you know. And we don't have a lot of money."

Has he lost it?

"Money? What does money have to do with anything?"

He sighs.

"We'll see, sweetheart. We'll see what the army can do for you. I know they'll do their best to look after a K-9 hero like you. And I'll speak to Diane. We'll look into crowdfunding. But in the meantime…."

He looks away. That's terrible news. Something wrong with Diane? Or the kids?

"What is it, Brown? What's the matter?"

"In the meantime, I'll have to start training a new dog."

13

I cock my head and stare at Brown, trying to understand what he said.

"A new dog? You want a new dog?"

Brown's face crumples like he's stepped on a nail, and the stench of guilt gets so intense it chokes me.

"See, Butter, I'm just a dog handler in the army. They need me back in Kandahar to keep our soldiers safe. I need to go back to work."

"Sure. Me too. We'll go back as soon as we get the prosthesis."

"There is no prosthesis, Butter."

"Not yet. But it's coming soon. We'll go back as soon as it arrives."

"Butter, the army can't wait. The soldiers are in danger now."

I sigh. Oh well. I guess I won't get to be Bionic Butter after all. It was nice while it lasted, imagining Viper's falling jaw and Guinness's delight. I'm a little sad, to be honest, since I really looked forward to, for once, stealing the show. Those two are so sharp and so competitive that I always feel like I'm last. It would be nice to be the best, just once. But it is what it is.

"Oh well. I hoped I'd show off to Guinness and Viper, but what can you do? I know they love me just the way I am, three-pawed and all. Let's go then."

"Butter, you can't go. You can barely walk a few feet. You can't work as an explosive detecting K-9 on three paws."

"I'll train, and I'll get better. And then, when the prosthesis arrives, maybe they can send it over."

Brown's eyes are bright with tears.

"Oh, Butter, how I wish that were possible. But it's not."

"What do you mean?"

"You have to stay here and get better. I'll speak to Diane about how we can get some money for the prosthesis. Maybe crowdfunding? One way or another, we'll get you that prosthesis as soon as we can."

"And then we go back to our war?"

Brown shakes his head.

"No, Butter, I don't think you'll ever go back to war. But I have to."

"But Brown, you know you can't sniff drugs! You can't even find your own stinky socks, even though I showed you a thousand times!"

"Butter, I'll have to... I'll have to get another dog."

The enormity of it crushes me. Brown wants another dog? How can that be? I've been with him my whole life. I know no other life but with him. And now, just because I lost a paw, he's going to leave me and get another dog? I don't get it. If Brown lost a leg, would I go get myself another human? Not in forever and a day. So how can he? My brain is not big enough to take this in.

"You mean you'll get another dog and go back to war?"

"After I train him, yes."

"And you'll go on patrol with Guinness and Viper? And your other dog?"

Brown nods, and I choke. This new dog will not only take Brown. He'll take my job and my friends. Viper, and even Guinness. Then what? What's left?

Brown tries to pet me.

"You'll be all right, Butter. You'll go home to Diane and the kids as soon as you're better. They're looking forward to having you back. And I'll call when I can."

"You'll call? You'll call from Afghanistan where you'll take the other dog?"

I stare at Brown's face, which held nothing but love for as long as I can remember, and I only see betrayal. My world just got upended, and the love fell out of it. I'm left with nothing. I thought it was bad when I lost my leg. It turns out that I was living the good life. Then, I still had people who cared for me. Now, I'm on my own. I hoped to be Bionic Butter, but it turns out I'll be just Lonely Three-Pawed instead.

I turn my back to Brown, and I lay my nose on my paw. Oh, how I wish I didn't wear my bulletproof vest the day I got shot. I wouldn't be here to listen to Brown talking about the other dog who'll take over my life. He'll have four paws, and Brown, and Viper and Guinness, while I rot here in this crate.

I've never been so miserable, not even when I got shot. Then, I had Brown and Guinness and Viper.

I've never hated anyone yet. But this new dog, I hate him. He took everything from me. I've got nothing left.

14

I didn't eat dinner that night. I couldn't sleep either. I just lay in my cell thinking about Guinness and Viper since I was too mad to even think about Brown.

I was flying to Afghanistan for my last deployment when I met Guinness. And I was bummed. Bad enough that I missed Diane and the kids already. But traveling as cargo? I was locked in a crate with nothing to do but listen to the engine noise and lick my paws. And I was desperate to pee.

I lay on one side; I rolled to the other; I crossed my legs. No good. I even tried to chase my tail to distract myself. Try that in a tight crate! Nothing helped. I couldn't stand it anymore, and I barked with frustration.

"What the fiddling funk!"

Far ahead, someone answered:

"Buddy?"

I was so relieved I almost peed myself.

"Who are you?"

"I'm Guinness. You?"

"I'm Butter. I need help!"

"What's up, Butter?"

"I'm hungry, I'm cold, and I need to pee."

"Same here. Just relax, buddy; we'll be there in no time."

"I can't relax. I need to pee."

"How about peeing in the crate?"

"I can't do that! I've never done it, not even when I was a pup."

I hear her mumble and fuss. Claws scratch the floor, then scrape metal. When I hear running water, I almost let go.

"Hey, Butter, are you a girl?"

"Of course."

"How about trying to pee like a boy? You know how they lift their leg and spray to the side? Try to pee through the grate. I just soaked a fancy golf bag smelling like cats, and it feels terrific."

I stare through my grate. Luckily, there's a pink Hello Kitty roll-on just ahead. Not as good as a real cat, but hey—beggars can't be choosers. Hello Kitty will have to do.

I turn sideways, balance on three legs, and let go, splashing the pink roll-on with the power of despair. Instant happiness courses through my body, and I can finally relax.

"That worked. Thanks, Guinness."

"Don't mention it."

That's Guinness. She's a rebel and a go-getter. And, despite her Teutonic pedigree, she's kind, funny, and sassy. I was ecstatic when we found out we were deployed at the same base in Kandahar.

My other best friend is Viper, and he's a different story. He's Belgian, a Malinois with a reputation to uphold. Have you ever met a Malinois? They're extreme athletes, intense, single-minded, and with a focus so sharp some call it neurosis. I once saw a Malinois jump on an IED and get himself killed just to prove a point. But that's not Viper. He isn't anything like that. Don't get me wrong now; he won't give you the warm fuzzies, and he won't tell you that you look thin when you're fat. But you can trust him to watch your back and tell you the truth whether you like it or not. He's strong, honest, and loyal, even though he's a little rough around the edges.

I wonder what they'll do when Brown shows up at the base with his new dog. Will they welcome and befriend him? Will they forget I ever existed? Or will they hold him at paw's length for the crime of stealing my life?

The thought of Guinness and Viper welcoming this imposter and sharing their lives with him makes me sick with loss and pain. The void in my heart hurts even worse than my missing paw, and I whimper.

"Butter?"

Nora's howl shakes the walls. Just one word, and every K-9 in the place is awake, wondering what's up. I'd love to pretend I'm asleep, but nobody would believe it. I sigh.

"Yes, Nora."

"I love you."

That came out of nowhere. We only met a few times in rehab. We barely know each other, and Nora's not into PDA. But her words find their way to my soul.

I sniff and mumble.

"Thank you, Nora."

Chorizo, the sausage dog to my left who never talks to anyone, sticks his long nose out through the grate.

"Love you, Butter."

My jaw falls. I occasionally spat some food toward his crate when I couldn't finish it, but we never talked. He never even thanked me.

"Love you, Butter."

That's Goldilocks, the Afghan hound in the crate kitty-corner from mine. He's an outcast. Target was the only one who ever spoke to him, but that's no wonder. Target would chat with a rock if he thought it needed a pick-me-up. That's the kind of dog Target is. Everyone else ignores Goldilocks. Not only because he's Afghan but also because of his long flowing hair, dark sultry eyes, and elegant silhouette. Goldie makes us all feel ugly and fat. I used to ignore him, too, until Target told me how heartbroken he is because his racing career is over. And, since he's Afghan and a hound, nobody wants him. I felt terrible, so I looked for something nice to say, but all that came to mind was the dust, the heat, and the IEDs. Then I remembered the Afghan food our translator once brought us.

"I love Kabuli palaw. Meaty rice, nutty pistachios, crunchy carrots, and especially the fried raisins topping. Mmm."

Goldie shook his head to uncover his eyes and looked at me.

"Really? My favorite is Qormah e Nadroo. Have you ever had it? Onions with yogurt, lotus roots, cilantro, and coriander. And lamb, of course."

After that, we exchanged recipes every once in a while. Now, as Goldie's smoldering eyes look at me with kindness and his mane floats around him like an aura, I'm so grateful I forget to be envious.

"Love you, Butter," someone says in the corner, and I don't even know who they are, but I love them too. I no longer feel lonely and useless. These are my people, and they care about me, even if Brown doesn't.

15

Life was on the up and up after that, even though I didn't forget about Guinness and Viper. Nor did I forgive Brown. I still felt rejected, but I no longer felt alone. With my new friends rooting for me, I gave my all to rehab, and I got waltzing pretty good.

"Good job, Three-Pawed. One of these days, they'll recruit you to *Dancing with the Stars*. I'd better teach you the samba while I'm still around," Nora says.

"Shut up, Nora." I stick my tongue out at her as she struggles to keep up with that treadmill that's way too slow for a drunk snail, but I know she's kidding. We're friends now, and she helps fill the void Brown left behind.

"What's the samba?"

"It's this Brazilian dance where you wear skimpy clothes, sway your hips, and shake your stuff."

"I don't have any stuff to shake."

"Many don't, but they shake it anyhow. It's all in the attitude."

That was all good fun, but I still couldn't climb stairs. My remaining front paw wasn't strong enough to hold me, and my balance wasn't good enough to let me do it on my hind legs alone. But I didn't give up. Day after day, I kept trying. Somewhere deep inside, I still hoped Brown was wrong, and if I worked hard enough, I could go back to work, even three-pawed as I was. But even I knew that to do that, I'd have to run, jump, and climb. Believe it or not, insurgents don't only place bombs where they're easy to reach. You need to look everywhere: under trucks, inside boxes, even on top of walls. And I couldn't even jump in a car.

The therapist watched me struggle with the stairs and sighed.

"It would help if you lost some weight, Butter."

My jaw dropped. I thought we were friends, and her words hit me right in the feels.

"Don't get me wrong now, pretty girl. I love you just the way you are. You're the best-looking three-pawed Labrador in the house. But, if you lost five pounds, you could do so much more."

"How do I do that?"

"You need to move more and eat less. But that's easier said than done."

She was right. I tried to leave some food in my bowl, but it kept calling my name until I licked the bowl clean. To help me out, they switched me to a low-calorie food that tasted healthy.

"Phew." Chorizo spat out the piece I'd sent him. "That's terrible. Is it vegan?"

"I dunno, but it's supposed to help me lose weight."

"It sure will. Don't send it to me anymore; it will ruin my appetite."

I kept trying, but I made little progress. Until one day, the therapist greeted me with a grin going from one ear to the other. She looked just like Target but for the black eye.

"Hey, Butter, I have a surprise for you."

My heart skipped a beat.

"I'm going back to work?"

"Not quite. But almost as good. Guess what?"

"What?"

"Your prosthesis arrived."

"My prosthesis?"

I'd been waiting for it for so long that I stopped hoping it would ever arrive. And now it had.

"Yep. Look!"

She opened a box full of bubbly plastic, the kind that sounds like a gunshot when you bite it. I totally love it, so I started bursting it until it sounded like a machine gun and half the gym dropped to take cover. She took it away.

"That's not what this is about, girl. Look."

She unwrapped a blue plastic contraption looking like a giant pizza wheel attached to a harness. I sniffed it, but I didn't smell any cheese—just chemicals.

"This is it?"

"Yep. Let's check it out."

She buckled the harness around my chest and adjusted it with the plastic wheel thing sticking out of my leg.

"Give it a try."

What the heck? I stood up and tried to waltz, but the wheel got in the way.

"Can you take out the wheel?"

"Nope. You've got to use it, Butter. Step on it. That's what it's for."

Use it? How do I use a pizza wheel when I don't have a pizza?

"Stop waltzing and try to tango. Instead of the 1-2-3, it's back to the old 1-2-3-4, my friend."

It's been so long, I forgot how to walk on four legs, but I tried. And go figure. Soon enough, I could walk and even run again! A little awkward at first, but I even got to climb a couple of steps by the end. Coming back down was another matter. I went helter-skelter and the thing twisted off.

The therapist gathered me off the floor and started unbuckling my new wheel.

"Wonderful job, Butter. I'm so proud of you! We'll do this again tomorrow."

"Can I please take it with me? Just for a moment? I want to show it to Nora and the others. They've been looking forward to it coming!"

"OK. But just for a moment."

She takes me back to the kennel, and I explode through the door barking up a storm.

"Hey, Nora, Goldie, Chorizo, look at this, will you? I'll introduce you to Bionic Butter!"

Silence. Nobody says anything. They stare at me with long mourning faces, then look away.

"What's wrong with you people? You don't like it? Is it because it's blue? You don't think blue looks good on me?"

Goldie clears his voice.

"It's very nice, Butter. Blue looks great on you."

"Very nice? Very nice? This is more than very nice. It's tremendous. Exciting. Stupendous. Formidable!"

"Yep."

"What the heck's wrong with you, people?"

Chorizo sniffs and Goldie follows suit.

"Nora died."

16

Nora, dead? I couldn't believe it, even though I knew Nora was dying even before I met her. Her spunk, her strength, her wisdom —where did they all go? Where do good dogs go when they die? And for that matter, where do people go?

I asked Chorizo and Goldie. They didn't know. I bet Nora did, but she wasn't saying.

The kennel wasn't the same without Nora. We all feared her howling and pointed words, but it turns out we all counted on her when things got rough. Whether we liked it or not, she nudged us to move forward instead of wallowing in self-pity. Just seeing that itsy-bitsy old dog stand at death's door with the strength of a hurricane made us ashamed to be weak.

Now that she was gone, we had to rely on ourselves. I worked hard on my rehab, and I got good at it. I could climb stairs almost as fast as I did when I had all my paws. I got so used to the funky-blue pizza cutter that I raced Goldie from one end of the gym to the other. He did three laps for each one of mine, and I still lost. How come, you ask? Well, why don't you try to keep up with an Afghan, for Dog's sake? They can run up to forty miles an hour. I could run maybe six for a minute or so, but that's just so I obey the speed limit. But at least I could run. Soon enough, I could go back to work, I thought.

I considered writing to Brown, even though I was still mad at him. He never came back to see me after the night he told me about The Other Dog. I thought I'd let him know that I was on the mend, and I'd soon be back to work, so he doesn't need The Other Dog. But I don't know how to write. And I didn't have his address. So I decided to wait until I was all better, then surprise him and Diane by walking home on my three paws and the pizza cutter.

"Where will you go? How do you know where your home is?" Goldie asked.

"I'll follow my nose, of course. How else? How do you know where to run?"

"I find things by sight. My nose isn't anywhere near my best feature," Goldie said, turning up his muzzle so we could all admire his elegant profile and silky ears.

Chorizo chuckled.

"Cut the crap, Goldie. We all know how pretty you are, and we're still your friends. Not because of it, but despite it."

Goldie's nose dove.

"I'm sorry; I just couldn't resist. You see, being pretty is all I've got—that, and my running. And I don't get much running these days. You all have something to be proud of. You, Butter, are a hero. You lost your leg while defending our country. You don't rub it in anyone's face, but we can all see you clawing your way through rehab just to go back to work. You, Chorizo, are a brave little soul, like all dachshunds. Your heart is larger than you are. Nora was our beacon of wisdom and honesty. Target has a heart of gold. He always has a good word for everyone, and he never failed to bring a smile to our faces. But me? I've got nothing but my speed and my looks. That's why I can't resist showing off every once in a while. It makes me feel like I'm worth something."

That made me sad. It's a sad day when you have to apologize for being pretty. And I know how much Goldie misses his freedom. His ancestors hunted the endless Afghan desert, but he's locked in a kennel no bigger than mine.

"Don't listen to Chorizo. He's just envious. We all are," I said.

But Goldie's luck was about to turn. One evening as we sat telling our stories, the vet brought someone to see Goldie. The visitor was a fancy man smelling like a forest in the rain who must have borrowed his clothes from a parrot.

We all stuck our noses out of our crates to sniff him better. None of us had been out in the rain for ages, and we missed it terribly, but he only had eyes for Goldie.

"Isn't he beautiful! Look at that silky golden coat!"

Goldie was delighted, but he's shy with strangers, so he shook his head, and his mane covered his eyes.

"Can he see?" Fancy asked.

"Of course. When he wants to."

"Can I see him better?"

The vet let him out, and Goldie got into it. His head high, his eyes sultry, he strutted his stuff and ran from one end of the kennel to the other, his golden locks floating behind him like a train.

Fancy picked his jaw off the floor.

"I'll take him."

"Take him? Take him where?" Chorizo yapped.

The vet nodded.

"He's a beauty, but he needs a lot of work. He needs to run every day for at least an hour in an enclosed space, otherwise he'll be gone. Jogging doesn't count. He needs to gallop to loosen his limbs, and no human can keep up with him."

Fancy shrugged.

"I have a large fenced yard. He can run all he wants for hours every day."

"His coat needs a lot of care. An hour a day or more, otherwise, it gets so matted it may never recover."

Fancy laughed.

"Don't you worry about that, Doc. Goldie's coat will have the best care money can buy. I'm a fashion photographer, and I need him to look phenomenal. Hey, Goldie, what would you think about starring in *Vogue*, my man?"

Goldie slobbered.

"What's *Vogue*?" I asked.

"The fanciest fashion magazine there is. One picture in it, and you've got it made," Goldie whispered, his eyes glued on Fancy's peacock blue coat. Fancy didn't miss it.

"You'll just strike a pose, and we'll have humans mesmerized. They'll slobber at the high heels, eyeglasses, and bags. What do you think?"

"Really?"

"Absolutely. I'll take care of everything. Your only job is to look fantastic and sell accessories. Deal?"

"You betcha."

When Goldie strutted out with Fancy, his head held high and his flowing tail following him, we watched him, torn between sadness and envy.

"We'll miss you, pretty boy!" Chorizo barked.

I sighed.

"It won't be the same without him, but at least he found a good fit."

Chorizo laid his nose on his paws.

"I always knew it's better to be pretty than to be smart."

I sighed.

"Our turn will be coming soon, sausage boy. Just hang in there. "

I wasn't really lying. I do wish Chorizo the best, but I hope I leave first. I'm so tired of the kennel, I can't deal with being alone again.

17

Days came and went; new dogs came and left, but Chorizo and I were going nowhere. We waited in the kennel for somebody to want us, but nobody did.

The hope that my prosthesis had revived faded away. I lost faith that I'd ever go back to work and be useful again. Nobody needed me.

My heart was no longer in rehab so I stopped pushing myself. My progress stalled, and it looked like I had reached my limit. Going back to work was just a pipe dream, so I resigned myself to being three-pawed forever.

Chorizo struggled too. Nobody wanted him either. We were like two inmates with no end in sight. So, since we had no future, we spent our time talking about the past. I told him about IEDs. He told me about badgers.

"That's what we, dachshunds, were bred for, hundreds of years ago in Germany. We were meant to dig into burrows and flush out badgers. That's why we're long, low, and stubborn. And brave, of course, but that goes without saying."

"Badgers? Why on earth would you want a badger? How do you cook them?"

Chorizo looked at me down his long nose, twitching his ears with impatience.

"For sport, of course. Badgers are fierce little creatures. Flushing them out of their burrows is not for the weak of heart; it takes courage and determination. Besides that, their hair is perfect for barber's brushes."

"Barber's brushes? Who uses them anymore?'

"Some purists still do. Badgers' hair is also good for paintbrushes. Anyhow, that's what we used to do, but that line of business is just about extinct. Nowadays, we're mostly pets."

I've heard of pets, but I've never been close to one. All my friends work for a living.

"What do pets do?"

"They wag their tails and eat snacks. They take their humans out for walks, then bring mud in the kitchen and eat the toilet paper."

"And then?"

"Then they nap and start over."

That didn't sound like fun.

"What work do they do?"

"That's just it: They don't work. Pets keep their humans company and make them happy."

"Sure, but I mean, what are they good for?"

Chorizo sighed.

"Oh, Butter. Once a K-9, always a K-9. How about trying to be just an ordinary dog for a change? Just chill, rest, and have fun?"

I didn't quite get it. But hey, to each their own. So when an elderly couple stopped by to see Chorizo and started babbling baby language to him, I bit my tongue instead of telling them off.

"What a cute little poopsy," the woman swooned.

"Yes. I'm cute. Really cute," Chorizo yapped, wagging his tail like crazy and laying on the charm.

"Poopsy!" I growled. They didn't hear me, but Chorizo did.

"Butter!"

"Yeah, yeah."

"That one's kinda noisy. How about this other one here?" the man said, bending over to stare at me.

The woman came to see me, and Chorizo's ears dropped.

"Poor doggy! He only has three legs. That's terrible! You're right; maybe we should take this one," she said, sticking her fingers in my crate to pet me.

Chorizo choked.

"Butter! You said you didn't want to be a pet!"

"What if I changed my mind?"

"But...but..."

"Just kidding, pal."

I bared my teeth and growled, and the woman pulled back faster than you could say pizza pie.

They left with Chorizo, of course. His short little legs moved a mile a minute, and his belly skirted the ground as he raced to the door.

He glanced back.

"Good luck, Butter. I love you."

"Love you too, pal. Have a good life."

And just like that, I was alone again. It wasn't new, but it was getting old. I had nothing left to fight for.

Some of the new dogs tried to be friendly, but I ignored them. You love them, and they leave, over and over again. I couldn't take any more heartbreak.

The therapist got worried.

"You've got to put your heart into your work, Butter; otherwise, nothing happens. You won't get better unless you try."

"Who cares? I'm doing nothing but lying in my crate all day anyhow."

"But Butter, you were doing so well. You made such progress. You can't stop now."

I did. I wanted nothing but to eat and sleep. My days of fighting were over.

The therapist told the vet.

"I think she's depressed. All her friends left, and she's still here."

The vet sighed.

"I'll see what I can do."

But nothing happened. I lay in my kennel, day after day, thinking about my friends. I wondered if Brown went back to Afghanistan with The Other Dog and if Guinness and Viper welcomed him. I thought about Target and his pangolins, about Goldie selling high heels on *Vogue*, about Chorizo bringing mud in his new kitchen. And about Nora, beyond the rainbow bridge.

That was the hardest. I missed Nora like crazy, but in a way, I was glad she wasn't there to see me. I knew she'd have a few choice words for me.

But one night she came to me in my dreams.

He ears hung close to the ground, but her fluttering wings kept her just high enough to ride that rainbow.

"Hey, you lazy Three-Pawed. Get off your butt and get moving, will you? You can't let yourself rot in that cage. You're a darn hero, remember? Act the part, for Dog's sake. Make me proud."

"But I don't have what it takes anymore. I spent it all."

"No, you didn't, you silly mutt. It's still right there, as long as you're willing to look for it."

"But Brown left me here. And all the others left. And nobody wants me."

"So what? Their loss. Get your rear in gear, you hear? Go do the work."

I did. Only because I was afraid that Nora would come back to berate me again. But I had no hope.

Then one day, the door opened.

"There she is!"

The voice sounded familiar, but I couldn't put my paw on it.

"Where?"

"There!"

I sniffed. The spicy aroma flooded my nostrils and lit up my brain. Cinnamon chili.

"Diane?"

"Butter!"

"Mom! Is it really you? And the kids!"

Diane and the kids hugged me and cried. I cried too, whimpering as I waltzed from one to the other. I licked their faces, I rolled on my back to let them scratch my belly, and then I hugged them again, trying to jump out of my skin.

"You're here! You came to see me!"

"Mom?"

"Yes, Aleta?"

"What happened to Butter's leg?"

"Butter worked with your dad in Kandahar. She got wounded as she took care of him."

Aleta kneels next to me, and her fingers trace the ugly scar below my shoulder.

"Will the leg ever grow back?"

Diane's voice cracks.

"No, it won't."

"But then, how will she walk?"

Diane blows her nose and looks away. I feel sorry for her.

"Oh, I can walk just fine. I can even run. Just wait until I show you my pizza cutter. I call her PC. "

Diane laughs and hugs me.

"So good to see you, Butter. We missed you terribly."

"I missed you too."

"OK, kids. It's time to go."

My heart skips a beat. They're leaving? Already?

"Go? Go where?"

"We're taking you home, Butter."

18

Home? Taking me home?

    I'm in such a rush to leave that I almost forgot my pizza cutter. I'm waltzing toward the door when the therapist catches me to buckle me in and show Diane how to adjust the harness.

    "It has to fit just right to take her weight evenly. If it slips, it will chafe and give her blisters."

    Aleta can't keep her hands off the buckles, struggling to fit it right, but BB cares more about the wheel-like foot. He tries to spin it and starts squeaking when it won't.

    The therapist lets me go, and I dash to the door, dragging Diane and the kids in my wake, worried they'll change their minds and leave me here. I push through the door, but it's clogged. The vet, the techs, and every other human in the hospital stands there in my way. I try to squeeze between their feet, but Diane pulls me back as they clap and start singing.

    "For Butter's a jolly good fellow,
    For Butter's a jolly good fellow,
    She's our own K-9 hero,
    And nobody can deny."

    They sound terrible, even though music is not my kind of art—

I'll take a pork schnitzel over a piano sonata any day of the week. But what's wrong with them? Have they gone rabid? I check, but they aren't foaming at the mouth, so why did they all lose their minds?

The vet comes over. I figure he wants to listen to my lungs, but no. He hangs a shiny tag on a purple ribbon around my neck.

"Congratulations, Corporal K-9 Butter. I am proud to present you with a Purple Heart medal for your heroism in battle and selfless sacrifice. Thank you for your service. May God bless you, and may God bless the United States of America."

The whole kennel goes nuts. They all bark and howl, even dogs I've never met.

"Well done, Butter, you three-pawed hero you!"

"Good luck, Butter."

"Keep up the good work, Sunshine."

"Catch a cat for me, will you?"

"We'll miss you."

I'm flabbergasted. I cock my head, staring from the dogs to the humans and back, wondering what hit them all, while Diane laughs so hard she's crying.

"They're honoring you, Butter. They're giving you the send-off a K-9 hero deserves. They all love you and wish you well."

I choke a little. I don't deserve it since I've been lazy, morose, and even rude to many. But I appreciate it. I lick my therapists' tears, and I bark goodbye.

"Thank you all. I'm so honored I don't know what to say. I wish you well."

I turn to Diane.

"Let's get out of here before they change their minds and keep me."

Home smells like vanilla, cinnamon, and basil, and it's covered with toys, shoes, and clothes scattered everywhere. I sniff everything from the front door to the large white bowl in the bathroom, looking for IEDs, but there aren't any. So I clean the cookie crumbs under the table and make a short job of the applesauce on the carpet before settling in the kitchen to supervise Diane's cooking.

I'm lying by the stove in a puddle of drool when Aleta drags me to her room to show me her latest drawing. Like really? Now, while Diane is cooking? These humans and their inedible arts! But the kid insists on pushing her picture in my face, so I glance at it just to humor her.

It's a yellow three-legged milking stool. I saw one just like that in Kandahar, and I was not impressed. This one, with three buckling legs and a sloping seat, looks even worse for the wear.

"Very nice," I lie, since you've got to encourage young creators.

"I made it for school."

"Really. Do you have goats there?"

"But I promised I'll bring you as soon as I can. They can't wait to see you in person."

Me? I do a double-take, and it dawns on me. That's not a milking stool. That's me.

Well then. The legs aren't that bad, but...

"You forgot the ears. And the tail."

She grabs a pencil, which happens to be black, and draws two triangles on top of the stool. I'd be darned if it doesn't look like Viper, with his sharp upright ears. Mine are yellow and flat.

She puts the black pen down and picks a green one to draw my tail. I shudder.

"They can't wait to meet a K-9 hero. I told them all about how you fought in the war and killed people and..."

"Not so fast, sparky. I didn't fight in the war, and I never killed anyone. I was just sniffing for IEDs, you know?"

"And I told them how you saved Daddy's life when you threw yourself between him and the bullet."

Where on earth is she coming from with this stuff?

"Now, wait a moment. Let's get it straight. I couldn't have jumped to take a bullet for Brown if I wanted to. And I didn't. I didn't even know a bullet was coming. If I'd known, I'd have run away."

"And they said they'll make you a cake and draw your picture."

The picture, I could do without. Between the milking stool and the green tail, my self-esteem hit rock bottom. But a cake?

"What sort of cake?"

"Strawberry cheesecake."

Well then.

"If you insist. But how about we skip the pictures?"

BB comes to lay on top of me and tickles my nose with his breath as he tries to spin my pizza wheel.

"You like it? Mom has one just like it, but smaller. I need this one, but you could take hers."

He ignores me and plays with PC until the harness buckles dig in my ribs and I have to stand. He shakes his finger at me.

"Doggy!"

"Mom! Mom!" Aleta shouts.

Diane rushes from the kitchen, her hands dripping with suds.

"What happened?"

"BB talked."

Diane's eyes widen.

"BB talked? Really? What did he say?"

"Doggy."

19

Being home with my family is everything I hoped for. That's what I dreamed about while I lay in my kennel, withering from the pain in my missing paw. That's what I looked forward to even when I was deployed with Guinness and Viper.

We lay in our crates waiting for dinner one evening. I was just chasing a nap when Guinness woke me up.

"What do you think will happen when this war is over?"

Now mind you, Guinness is as bright as a dog can be, and she's the best K-9 I ever met but for Viper. And even that's debatable. But she's still green. That was her first deployment, and she still hoped, like all youths do, to change the world and make it better.

But that one came out of left field. So much so that Viper forgot about cleaning his privates to stare at her.

"I would not worry about that. Once started, wars last forever. The one thing we have here, besides dust, is job security."

"I wasn't worried, just curious. What would we do if the war were over? What would you do, Butter?"

"I'd like to get home to Diane and the kids. I'd supervise her cooking, clean up the spills, and help her test new recipes. I'd play with the kids, take them out for long walks, and bark at the mailman. And clean up the house of food crumbles. Or something along those lines."

"How about you, Viper?"

"That is an entirely hypothetical question that I do not intend to entertain at this point, hein?"

Guinness cocked her head, then looked at me for a translation.

"He doesn't think that's gonna happen anytime soon, so he says you shouldn't worry about it. He thinks the war is here to stay."

"Common, Viper, work with me here for a moment. What about if they sent us home tomorrow. What would you do?"

Viper sighs.

"I would just do what they needed me to, which is most likely that I would go to fight the next war."

"But what if there was no war?"

"There will always be wars."

"But just for the sake of it, say there was no war for a year. What would you do?"

"That is a silly presumption, really. But I would sniff explosives for the TSA to curb terrorism, or I would work for the police, looking for firearms and perpetrators. But do not hold your breath,

Guinness. The war is here to stay. But say you were right, and the war was suddenly over. What would you do if you had a choice, *hein*?"

Guinness shrugs like she's never thought about that, even though she kept harassing us.

"I'd go with Silver wherever she goes, and I'd look after her. She's got no one else, and she's my responsibility."

That got us all thinking. We were all so different, even though we all did the same job. Viper was obsessed with his work, I was committed to my family, and Guinness was devoted to her human.

"What if there was no Silver to look after?"

Guinness sat up straight, piercing Viper with narrowed eyes.

"What are you saying, Viper?"

"Say something happened to Silver, and she was no longer your problem. What would you do next?

"Nothing will happen to Silver as long as she's my responsibility. I'll take care of her."

Viper sighed.

"Guinness, I have been a K-9 for more years than you have been alive. Sabrina is my fourth handler. One quit, one retired, one died. Things happen in war. They happen to dogs and to people. You cannot build your whole life around a human, or you will get burned."

Guinness flattened her ears and laid her nose on her paws. When she finally answered, she woke me up from my nap.

"I don't know, Viper. I hate to see your point, but I do. Shorty, my first handler, was a great guy. He trained me and loved me. I was his partner and his family. I thought we'd be together forever until one night, he died in his sleep. Then the Army set me up with Silver. I was lucky that she's a good human and worth looking after. So, when it's all said and done, I guess I'd find another human to take care of."

Then dinner came. It was chicken, so I got busy eating, and I don't know what else those two talked about, but I'll never forget that night. Viper lives for his job, Guinness is devoted to her human, and I am committed to my family.

It's good to be home.

20

Diane, the kids, and I soon settled into a nice routine. I take them for a walk in the morning; then we drop the kids at school. I look after the house while Diane goes to work. After we get the kids from school, we take them to the park. I've been working on teaching them how to sniff the news at every mailbox, signpost, and the better bushes, but it's a slow go. Sniffing doesn't look like their thing. They're pretty good with the ball, though. They throw it, I catch it, and then they chase me to get it back. Great fun!

When we go home, Diane cooks dinner, and I supervise. She's lucky to have me taste her new recipes. She said nobody in the house has a palate like mine. Of course not. Flavor is all about the smell, and nobody has a nose like mine, certainly not the kids. BB still doesn't know when he pooped, even if I can smell it from the basement.

These kids, bless their hearts, aren't easy to feed. Diane composes these delicious creations with luscious sauces and crispy grilled vegetables—I'm particularly partial to asparagus with Hollandaise sauce. It's so good it doesn't even taste like a vegetable, but that's not the best part. The best part is the social interaction.

Asparagus makes your pee smell amazing, and every dog in the neighborhood comes to check it out.

"You had asparagus again, didn't you?" the wiry terrier down the road asks, leaving his mark next to mine.

I sniff it.

"Small breed hypoallergenic? Really? That's the best you can do?"

But that's unfair. Wiry's human is not a chef, and I bet he does the best he can. But I digress.

My point is that Diane cooks all these yummy dishes, and the kids want nothing but pizza and PBJ sandwiches. Especially BB, who goes into a meltdown whenever Diane tries to feed him something new. He drifts into a world of his own that none of us can reach.

"You should try feeding them MREs. That would teach them," I said when he blew up because she'd undercooked his egg.

But she laughed and kept cooking, and I kept on eating. Life was good.

I wondered where Brown was, but I didn't want to ask. Truth be told, I didn't really want to know, just in case he was with The Other Dog. Until one day, Aleta spoke to him, then jumped up with excitement.

"Daddy's coming home!"

"Really? When?"

"Tomorrow."

Diane turned the whole house upside down. She vacuumed under the sofa and threw away every one of my old marrow bones; I had to recover them from the trash and hide them. There wasn't much left on them, but they still had emotional value, eh? She told the kids to clean up their rooms—that was worth watching—then cleaned up after them. She even brushed me.

I crawled under the bed, but crawling is the one thing Pizza Cutter doesn't excel at, so she caught me.

I tried to parlay my way out of it.

"You don't need to bother. Brown has seen me even worse. After looking for IEDs in Kandahar, I was so dusty you couldn't tell me from the background."

You think she listened? Neh. She even cleaned the inside of my ears and trimmed my nails. She tried to brush my teeth, but that's where I drew the line. I hid under the table and growled until she gave up and went to take a shower.

I try to act cool, but I'm terribly excited. I'm half hopeful and half scared. I haven't seen Brown since he told me about The Other Dog, ages ago. Since then, I've made tremendous progress. I can walk, run, and even jump. I know he'll be surprised. But am I good enough?

I cleaned my privates really well, and I looked for something fragrant to roll in, but I didn't find much—just a smidge of duck poop in the park - but I made the most of it.

Diane gasped. Her eyes grew big as saucers.

"What are you doing, Butter! And I don't have time to give you a bath!"

"Good."

I kept away, so she couldn't smell me. Fortunately, she was so busy she forgot.

It was almost dark by the time we got ready. The house smelled of rosemary, garlic, and thyme; the kids were clean; and Diane had put on lipstick and perfume. I, for one, don't think much about perfume. I'd find her sexier if she rubbed herself with the roast, but hey. What do humans know about smells?

"How much longer, Mom?" Aleta asked.

"Any moment now."

The doorbell rang, and the kids ran to the door.

"Daddy, daddy!"

"Aleta. BB."

I hear them hug and kiss, but I can't see them since I was too chicken to join them. I hid in the bathroom instead.

"Joe! You're back!"

More hugging and kissing.
"Where's Butter?" Brown asks. "I have something for her."
For me? Something for me?
I dash out.
"I'm here."
Brown hugs me, and all is right with the world.
Then he says:
"Butter, meet your sister, Lovely."

21

My sister, Lovely?

I cock my head to understand.

When I finally do, my heart blows up like I've stepped on an IED. Or is it my brain?

Lovely? Really?

My hackles go up as The Other Dog steps forward from behind Brown.

I should have sniffed her long ago, but I was so excited about seeing Brown that I lost my common sense. I stare at her in horror as she wags her tail and leaps toward me.

"Hey, Butter, old girl! I couldn't wait to meet you! Brown told me all about you, from when you guys used to work together. Remember when you stole a chicken bone, then puked it all over his best shirt?"

She puts on the charm, wagging her tail and acting playful. Then she proceeds to sniff my butt.

Are you kidding me? This interloper wants to sniff my butt FIRST? When she's not only an intruder in my home, but she's just a pup? I'm so outraged that I bare my teeth and growl as if I'm ready to rip her throat open. She whimpers, squeezes her tail between her legs, and hides behind Brown. I leap to get her.

"Butter! Stop it!"

Diane is horrified. Me too, just not for the same reasons. I stare at Brown.

"How could you?"

He looks away. Diane may be surprised, but he's not. Brown knew he was breaking my heart, but he still got The Other Dog and named her Lovely. He could at least call her Fatty, or Poopsy, or Blubber, but no. He had to call her Lovely. That takes the cake.

And what makes it worse is that she is lovely. She's a beautiful Springer Spaniel with long caramel ears and come-hither brown eyes. And she stinks.

"Look at her. Isn't she cute?" Diane asks, leaning over to pet her.

"Cute? Are you out of your mind? She's The Other Dog. She stole Brown, she stole my job, she stole my life. You call that cute?"

Brown eyes me wearily.

"Butter may need some time to adjust. She's used to being an only dog, you know, and she's gone through a lot. We may need to work on socializing her."

I blow up.

"Me? An only dog? How about Viper and Guinness? How about Nora and Chorizo and Target and the rest? I'm plenty socialized, thank you very much. You go socialize your Other Dog and leave me alone."

Brown sighs.

"I guess we'll have to give them time."

Believe it or not, dinner that evening wasn't fun. The Other Dog curled under Brown's chair. I watched her like a hawk, growling like a chainsaw whenever she moved. She dropped her ears and looked away, pretending she didn't notice me, but I made sure she knows whose home this is.

Later on, when she tried to explore the house, I made it clear that she should keep her nose to herself. Diane held me while Brown showed her around. She sniffed everything, her little tail quivering as she moved from one room to the next while I watched, my blood boiling with anger. She even dared to smell Aleta's tripod drawing.

"Don't touch that, you stinky long-eared imposter," I growled. That's mine!"

"Come on, Butter. She's not hurting anything! Be nice! She's your sister!"

"My sister? Are you nuts? What would you say if Brown brought home another woman and told you to welcome her as a sister?"

Diane's face fell.

"If you put it that way...."

After dinner, we sat watching each other as if at a wake until Brown couldn't take it anymore.

"Let's take them for a walk. That helps shape a pack. Common purpose and all that."

We filed out, Brown and Other first, then the kids holding hands, then me, with PC and Diane. I had cooled down a little by then, so I tried to show Brown how well I was doing. I walked, I ran, I even jumped, but he didn't notice. He only had eyes for The Other. He talked to her, petted her, and rewarded her for every stupid little thing. He even called her a "Good Girl" for coming when he called her. Sickening!

Diane tried to help.

"That's OK, Butter. He needs to train her. Remember how he trained you when you were a just pup?"

"I remember. Does he?"

Diane sighed.

"He still loves you, Butter. He loves you just as much as he always did, but she's his work partner. He needs to teach her and train her."

"I'm his work partner."

Diane hugged me and wiped her eyes. We both know I'm no longer Brown's partner. The Other is. I'm just useless Three-Pawed.

That night I slept with Aleta while Brown and The Other slept in Diane's bedroom. And I couldn't help but hear them talk.

OK, OK, I strained my ears to listen. So what? Wouldn't you?

"I don't like how this is going," Brown said. "I was afraid Butter wouldn't welcome Lovely, but I didn't think she'd try to kill her."

"Give them some time, Joe. Remember that Butter has been through a lot. She's just settled back home, and all of a sudden, there's this other dog who took her place and is about to take over her home. Of course, she's upset. Give them some time to work things out."

"What if they don't?"

"They will. We'll do our best to get them adjusted. We'll get a trainer, and...."

"I am a trainer."

Diane sighed.

"You're training them to detect explosives, not to get along. We'll find a K-9 behaviorist who specializes in that. Like Cesar and others. We'll get help."

"You know we don't have that kind of money. That prosthesis alone cost us an arm and a leg."

"Come on, Joe. It will be all right. Butter is nothing but love and loyalty. We'll find a way to make them get along. Just give them time."

"What if they don't?"

Diane sighed.

"I don't know, Joe. Do you?"

"If they don't learn to get along, Butter will have to go."

I have to go? Go where? This is my only home other than the base in Kandahar. And that war is over for me.

I have nowhere to go.

22

Things didn't get any better. If anything, they got worse.

Brown acts like I don't exist. He only pays attention to Lovely. They go training every day while I stay home to look after the house. He doesn't speak to me, of course. But I can smell the TNT, the fertilizer, and the plastique on them when they come back home.

He only talks to Lovely, plays with her, and trains her. And I know he does it on purpose. So does Diane. I hear her speak to him one night.

"Listen, Joe, what you're doing is wrong. You can't treat Butter like she's useless. That's no good. You need to spend time with her too. Make her feel loved."

"There's only so much I can do. Lovely needs my attention. The pup has a great nose and excellent work ethic, but she's got a lot to learn before we get deployed. Plus, Butter needs to come back to her senses. She's been acting like a spoiled brat. She will get attention when she behaves like a good dog."

I don't want to be a good dog. I want to be a killer. Seeing this thief take over my life makes me boil inside. But there's nothing I can do but watch her win their hearts. BB spends hours combing his fingers through her long silky ears. Aleta plays with her while I lie morose in a corner, watching them. Even Diane likes her and gives her tasty treats when she thinks I'm not watching.

The Other Dog stole not only my job; she stole my family, and I hate her guts. I'd love to kill her, but I'm not a killer. I'm just a peaceful Labrador who never killed anyone beyond a few flies. So, instead of killing, I just withdraw into myself as I watch her take over my life. There's a painful void in my soul, and the only thing that fills it is food. I eat more and more, even though I shouldn't, but nothing else helps me through this misery.

I'm in my corner with my tail covering my eyes, trying to sleep, when I hear Aleta ask Diane:

"Can I take Butter to school tomorrow for show and tell? My teacher said we can have a party for her."

"That may do her good. What do you think, Butter? Would you like a party?"

I turn away. I don't want a party. I just wish Lovely would disappear.

"Come on, Butter, you'll enjoy it."

"No."

Aleta's eyes fill with tears.

"Butter, you promised! Remember when I told you they can't wait to meet you? And they'll draw your picture?"

"You said cheesecake. Strawberry cheesecake."

"Of course."

What can a K-9 do, faced with a crying little girl and the promise of strawberry cheesecake? I sacrificed myself, and I agreed.

The following morning, Diane brushed me well, fitted my pizza cutter, and hung my purple tag around my neck. Aleta took me to her class, and that was something else.

If you thought going to war is terrible, just try going to kindergarten!

I'd never seen so many kids screaming, running, and jumping.

It's total chaos, and I'm about to run away when they see me and freeze in place.

Aleta walks me and PC to the front of the room. We sit while Aleta introduces us.

"This is Butter. Butter is a K-9 corporal hero. She got deployed in Afghanistan, where she detected explosives that can hurt people. Then she got wounded and received this purple medal. Her leg was destroyed, so they had to cut it off, but then she got a prosthesis and learned to walk again. Now she can walk and even run. Sometimes she even jumps."

"Very nice, Aleta," the teacher says. "Butter, thank you so much for coming. Kids, do you have any questions?"

A red-headed kid raises his hand.

"What sort of dog is Butter?"

"She's a Labrador."

"Can all Labradors find bombs?"

"Only if they are specially trained."

"Where is her leg now?"

"Her leg is gone, but the scientists made this replacement, and she's just as good as new."

"What does she eat?"

Now we're talking. Where's my cheesecake?

It took a while to get to the cheesecake. Every kid came to pet me, talk to me, and check out my pizza cutter. I sat for them to draw me, and they showed me their drawings. All I can say is WOW! I'd never have known that was me if they didn't tell me. But they meant well, and they were cute. And when we finally got to the cheesecake, I got two servings, plus the clean-up. All in all, I'd call it a success.

A little blonde girl comes to say goodbye as we're leaving. Aleta introduces her.

"This is Mia. She's my best friend."

Mia offers me a strawberry. I lick the frosting and try to avoid the red part without hurting her feelings. But she won't take no for an answer.

"It's good for you. It has vitamins and minerals that help you heal, my Mom says, and she's a doctor. I saved it especially for you."

Oh well. I do my best to swallow it without tasting it, but I still pucker from its tartness.

I lick Mia's fingers to say thanks, and she turns to Aleta.

"You're so lucky to have a friend like Butter. She's a hero, and she's beautiful. We only have cats. Would you like to switch?"

Aleta shakes her head but beams with pride. So do I. For the first time in a while, I don't feel worthless. What a good day!

Then we went home.

23

I knew something was wrong the moment Diane picked us up from school. Her eyes were red and swollen, and she smelled damaged. Kind of like I did when I lost my leg. So, I checked her legs. They were there, just two of them, as usual. She didn't even limp, but I knew something was wrong.

She didn't even ask how the show-and-tell went. But then she didn't need to. Aleta didn't stop talking all the way home.

"My friend Mia said that Butter is not only beautiful, but also a hero, and how happy we must be to have a dog like her. They only have two cats who never do anything but sleep. She said she'd trade both cats for Butter. She'd throw in her bike and even the helmet, but I said no. I don't know how to ride a bike anyhow. We had cheesecake, and Kirk dropped his to the floor, but Butter cleaned it up."

Diane nodded. Once in a while, she'd glance at us through the rear-view mirror. Her blotched face looked sadder than I've ever seen it since Brown took me to war.

We got home, and the kids settled in the living room. Aleta undressed her doll while BB spun the wheels of his toy truck as usual. Diane started cooking dinner, but she was so distracted she forgot to put garlic in the tomato sauce, but she salted it twice. She was just about to do it again when I stopped her, but it was too late. That sauce was terrible.

I was so worried about her that I got in her way at every step, sniffing for an explanation. She didn't smell sick, just upset and dejected, so I had a thought.

"Did Brown get you a sister wife?"

Diane covered her face with her hands, and I didn't know if she was laughing or crying.

But it didn't matter. I lay my head in her lap and licked her nose, and she wiped her eyes and stroked my ears.

"Oh, Butter, it's terrible."

"What happened?"

"I was…"

The front door creaked open. Brown and Lovely were back, so I slid under the table to avoid them.

Brown saw Diane and gasped.

"What happened?"

"BB."

"BB? What about him? I just saw him; he looks fine."

"He had his annual check-up today. His doctor is worried about him."

"Why?"

"At his age, he should be speaking, but he barely responds to his name. He also makes little eye contact and doesn't play with others, so she thinks he may be on the spectrum."

"What spectrum?"

"Autism spectrum. She wants BB to see a developmental specialist."

"What for?"

"To get him help. All kids with autism have trouble communicating. They start speaking late, if at all, and struggle with new situations. But they're all different. There's no telling how BB will progress, but the sooner he gets help, the better his chance to live a normal life."

I lie under the table, struggling to understand, but I can't. The one thing I get is that they're worried about BB. I can't imagine why. He's a sweetheart unless Diane pours his milk in the wrong glass or tries to brush his hair. But otherwise, he's so loving, he'd spend hours running his fingers through my tail.

Brown sobs.

"That can't be true. Not my boy! Not BB!"

I'm about to crawl out from under the table to lick him and make him feel better when I see Lovely put her pretty little paws on his knees and lick his face.

I lie back. Brown doesn't need me; Lovely has him covered.

But Diane and BB do.

24

A few days later, I watch Diane get ready to leave, and I crawl in my corner, feeling sorry for myself. But instead of saying goodbye, she harnesses my pizza cutter and clips my leash, then wipes off my boogers and scratches my ears.

"We're going on a visit today, so you need to look pretty."

"Who are we visiting?"

"A sick kid. His name's Tariq."

"Why?"

"His doctor is Mia's mother. Mia told her about you, and she thinks you could help him."

"With what? Does he need to look for explosives?"

"I don't think so, but we'll find out."

We drive to a small house at the other end of town. A tiny woman dressed in black opens the door, letting out a waft of exciting aromas: Cumin, cardamom, and coriander hit my nose and make me drool. I try to follow the scent to the kitchen to investigate the situation, but Diane holds me tight and we follow the woman to a crowded blue room.

A massive metal bed swallows the room, making the boy in it look small. He's pale, bald, and too busy with his tablet to look up.

"Tariq, this is Butter. She came to see you."

"Yep."

"Tariq!"

"Hi, Butter."

Tariq's eyes stay glued to his tablet while his narrow fingers tap on it like hail.

His mother sighs.

"Why don't we give them a moment? How about a cup of coffee?"

"Sure," Diane says.

They leave, and the door closes before I can follow, so I stand wondering what to do. Tariq has no use for me. His doctor was mistaken.

I watch him play on his tablet until I get bored. Then, since I've got nothing better to do, I start sniffing around for IEDs. You never know. There's no trace of explosives, but I find some cookie crumbs under the bed and I clean them up.

I try to crawl under the bed to look for more, but crawling is the one thing PC isn't great at, so I'm still struggling when Tariq calls.

"Butter?"

Oops. I flatten my ears.

"I was just checking, you know. Making sure there are no IEDs and such. I only found the cookies by mistake."

"What happened to your leg?"

"Oh, that? I got shot."

"You got shot?"

"Yep. In Afghanistan."

Tariq puts his tablet aside.

"What were you doing in Afghanistan?"

"I was a K-9, detecting explosives with my friends Guinness and Viper."

"Did you find any?"

"Explosives? Of course. There were plenty. More than anyone could want."

"What did you do with them?"

"Nothing. I just pointed them out to Brown. He told the team, and they defused them."

"Does your leg hurt?"

"Not anymore. It did when I got shot, but then they cut it off and gave me this pizza cutter instead."

"May I see it?"

"Of course."

He studies the harness, then the wheel.

"Does it work?"

"Like a charm. After they cut my leg, I had to waltz on my three legs, but now I can tango. I can even run and climb stairs."

"Don't people stare at you when they see you?"

"Sure, they do. So what?"

"You don't mind being stared at?"

"Not in the least. I see it as a compliment. If people didn't like me, they'd look elsewhere."

Tariq leans back.

"Really! I never thought about it that way."

I cock my head.

"What other way is there?"

"Like, you are not like the others. You're less than the others."

"I'm not less than the others. I am more. I am me, and also PC."

Tariq laughs like he forgot how it's done.

"PC?"

"Yep. Pizza Cutter. That's what I call my prosthesis."

"You like it?"

"Are you kidding? I love it. With it, I get to be Bionic Butter. Without it, I'm just Three-Pawed."

Tariq stares at PC for a long time. Then he glances at me.

"You know, Butter, I also lost my leg."

"Really? How could you lose it? Wasn't it attached?"

He laughs again, easier this time.

"I mean, they had to cut it off."

"I see. Just like mine. You got shot?"

"No."

"What happened to you?"

"I got osteosarcoma. That's a sort of cancer."

My tail hides between my legs. Cancer is terrible. That's what Nora died from, but she got it from having all those litters. Tariq doesn't look like breeding stock, but who knows?

"What happened? You had puppies?"

"No. I had cancer. It's like a disease."

"I know. How did you get it?"

"I don't know. But they had to cut my leg to stop it from spreading to the rest of my body and killing me."

"Oh, good. So it's gone now?"

"Yes. But so is my leg."

"That's OK. You can get a new one. Maybe they can make you a pizza cutter like mine."

"I don't want a pizza cutter."

"Why not?"

He looks at PC, and I know he's about to say something nasty, but he refrains.

"I just want my leg back."

I don't know what to say. Fortunately, I don't have to say anything since the door opens and Diane comes in.

"Time to go, Butter. We need to get the kids from school. Nice meeting you, Tariq."

"Thanks for stopping by," Tariq's mother says. "Please come back soon."

"Bye," Tariq says, his eyes back to his tablet.

25

Diane cried all the way back. She's still upset after we pick up the kids, and she sets them to play in the living room.

She sniffs as she starts on a coconut curry, and I lie by the stove to support and supervise her. And clean up the spills, of course.

"Like learning that your kid has cancer wasn't bad enough! They had to amputate his leg. And after all that, to watch him wither. That poor woman, I don't know how she does it."

I cock my head.

"What does she do?"

"Oh, Butter, you don't understand. There's nothing harder for a mother than to watch her child suffer and be unable to help. It's terrible."

She stirs the coconut milk in the frying aromatic spices, and I start drooling. It's not that I don't care; I care very much. But the food smells terrific, I'm starving, and there's nothing I can do for Tariq. The kid will have to work his way through this mess by himself like I did.

"That poor kid! He won't go out, he won't see his friends, he won't try his prosthesis. He hides in his room, since he doesn't want anyone to see he's disabled."

I swallow my slobber while looking out for any drips from her spoon, ready to catch them on the fly. With these things, you can never be too careful. But I feel her pain.

"That's what I thought too. But it makes no sense whatsoever. Why would you be embarrassed by something that's not your fault? I understand being ashamed of doing something wrong, like pooping inside, chewing the tips of Brown's shoes, or stealing someone's life. But why would you be ashamed of something that's not your fault? You, humans, are weird."

"That's why I thought meeting you could help him. You have such a healthy way of dealing with your disability, Butter. I hoped some of it would rub off on Tariq. You aren't embarrassed to be missing your leg, are you?"

"Are you kidding? I'm proud of PC, and I'm happy to show it off. It's not quite like having a real leg, especially when you crawl. But if I had my leg, I'd be in Kandahar sniffing for IEDs instead of being home supervising dinner. Anyhow, it is what it is. I might prefer things to be different, but they are what they are. And I have nothing to be ashamed of."

Diane stops stirring to stare at me.

"You miss Afghanistan, Butter?"

"I don't miss the dust, the MREs, and the heat."

"But?"

"I miss my friends, Guinness and Viper. I miss being part of a team working to protect our people. I miss being useful."

"But you're useful here. We love you."

I sigh.

"I love you too."

A drop of curry falls to the floor, and I clean it up.

"How is it?"

"Not enough to tell."

She pours some in my bowl. I sniff it carefully. The rich aroma of curry, coconut, cilantro, and cinnamon bathes my nostrils, sending me into a drooling frenzy. I taste it.

"A bit more salt, maybe. And a touch of shrimp paste."

Diane tastes it too.

"I'd be darned if you aren't right. You should be a professional taster, Butter."

"Now that's a job I'd do for love."

It felt good to chat, just the two of us like we used to when I had all my legs and there were no intruders in the house. But it didn't last long. That evening, over dinner, Diane told Brown about Tariq.

"The poor kid's so distraught he won't even look at his prosthesis, let alone use it. And his mom is at the end of her rope. That's why Mia's mom sent us there. She thought that if Tariq sees how well Butter does with her prosthesis, he may give his a try."

"Did it help?"

"I don't know. He didn't seem interested."

"Maybe he just needs time."

"Maybe."

"How about talking to his mother about giving them Butter?"

Diane's spoon clangs as it drops on her plate. Curled under Brown's chair, Lovely wags her tail. My jaw drops.

"How about doing what?"

"Well, it sounds like they could use Butter. We have no use for her. Wouldn't it be great to have some peace if she weren't here to harass Lovely all the time?"

"Are you kidding?"

"Not in the least."

Diane raises her voice.

"How can you say that, Joe? Butter lost her leg to keep you safe. And you want to discard her like a used napkin? I hope you're a better man than that."

"But Diane, it would be for her own good. She's not happy here. She may be happier as an only dog."

Lovely wags her tail and snickers at me. I bare my teeth and growl, but she won't back down. She does the "Nah-Nah-Nah-Nah-Nah-Nah" victory dance, and I lose it. I leap from my spot under Aleta's chair, grab Lovely by the scruff of her neck, and shake her like a ripe fruit tree. She squeals bloody murder, but I won't let go. I've had enough.

"Let her go! Let her go!"

Let her go? Are you kidding me? I bite even deeper, filling my mouth with her fur like Guinness taught me, until I taste her blood.

The kids scream. Brown tries to pull me away, but I won't let go. I growl like a lawnmower. Lovely squeals. Diane cries.

Brown kicks me in the face.

I'm so mad that I can't see straight. A red veil covers my eyes, and I can't see anything but the rage consuming me. And Brown's angry eyes.

I let go of Lovely, and I bite him.

26

I was a bad dog. I deserve to be in jail.

I'm locked in my crate. I've been here for days now, waiting for my sentence. And one thing is sure: It won't be pretty.

Biting Lovely was bad enough. But biting Brown? There's no worse sin other than biting one of the kids. Everything else—pooping indoors, eating shoes, even stealing someone's life—pales by comparison. My name is Butter, and I'm a criminal. I lie in my crate with my ears so flat they're like gone, my tail tucked between my legs and my heart full of remorse. I was a bad dog.

Lovely cherishes every moment, and she stops by my crate every once in a while to snicker at me. She's got a tidy row of stitches. As far as she's concerned, it was all worth it. A few stitches and she's got the whole family on her side. Brown hasn't even glanced at me since he locked me up. The kids aren't allowed to talk to me. The only one who still speaks to me is Diane, but she's not happy with me either. Whenever she brings me food or takes me out, her eyes are dark with worry.

"You shouldn't have done that, Butter. It's not Lovely's fault you lost your leg and can no longer go to war, and it's not Brown's fault that he has a job to do. He must train her. He could be more sensitive, but that doesn't excuse what you did. You're in BIG trouble."

"I know."

"Will you do it again if he lets you out?"

I wish I could say no, never, but I'm not so sure. I don't know what I'll do if Lovely provokes me again or if Brown kicks me.

"I don't know."

She locks me back in my crate, but that evening I hear her talk to Brown.

"We need to let Butter out. She's been locked up for days."

"So? You know what she did. You can't let her out since you can't trust her. Not only with Lovely but even with us. Especially with the kids."

"That's silly, Joe. Butter loves the kids. She's looked after them since they were born, and she's never hurt them. Aleta loves her, and BB is so much easier to handle when he's with Butter. You know that as well as I do."

"I know nothing except that she bit Lovely so ferociously that it cost us three hundred dollars that we don't have to get her stitched. And she bit me. What's she going to do next time she's in a rage?"

"Joe, she can't live in that crate forever."

"She won't have to. I'm working on it."

"What are you working on?"

"On rehoming her."

"You're still thinking about giving her to Tariq's mom?"

"I wish. You can't place an aggressive animal in a home with a disabled kid. I'm looking for a home with no pets and no kids, willing to take on an old, disabled, dangerous dog. It's not easy, believe me."

"What will happen if you can't find it?"

"We'll talk about it when the time comes."

"Let's talk about it now."

"I'll work harder."

"And if you still don't?"
"If I don't, we'll have to put her down."

27

"Put her down," Brown said.

Me? Put me down? Down where?

I struggle to understand what he means, but I can't. Brown's words turn over and over in my mind. They make no sense. Where will they put me? Then I remember Viper's twin.

It was hot that evening, like every other evening in Kandahar. Guinness, Viper, and I lay panting in our crates, talking about the days of our youth. The soldiers played cards at the other end of the hangar. Then somebody turned up the music, and Gotye's "Somebody that I Used to Know" blasted from the radio.

"Now and then, I think of when we were together.
I told myself that you were right for me
But felt so lonely in your company
But that was love, and it's an ache I still remember."

Viper's ears went up like the music stirred something in him. He sighed and lay his nose on his paws.

"That used to be his favorite song. My brother Jinx and I were twins, you know. We both enrolled in the military. We trained together and passed every test with flying colors. Looking at him was like looking in a mirror. We always tried to outdo each other, but it was darn hard since we were both so good."

His amber eyes shone as he looked somewhere in the past. Guinness and I sat up to listen since Viper rarely talked about himself.

"Who was better?" I asked.

"Sometimes me, sometimes him. Jinx was fast, sharp, and tireless."

"You sound like you're talking about yourself," Guinness said.

"He was all that and more. Our handlers could not tell us apart. We were microchipped, of course, so there was a way to tell who was who, but not by watching us work, *hein*?"

"Did you guys ever switch trainers just for laughs?" Guinness asked.

Viper's jaw dropped.

"How did you know?"

"I didn't. But I would have if I had a chance."

"We did. One day we switched trainers. I went to his home, and he went to mine. We pretended we knew everyone and acted as if we belonged there. It was fun to sneak like that in the home of a stranger, acting like I knew everyone, even though I had never seen them. I did not know where to find the water dish or where pooping happened, but I managed. No one noticed, but...."

"But who?"

"Jinx's cat, Turbo. He was a stray tabby Jinx had found in the street. They called him Turbo because he purred like an overcharged engine. That is probably because he was deaf, and he could not hear himself. Turbo and Jinx grew up together, played together, and ate together. They were inseparable."

"Really? A Belgian Malinois and a cat?"

"Yep. Weird, I know. Jinx was fond of Turbo, and Turbo loved Jinx. They slept together in the same bed and shared a language their humans did not know. So, that evening when I went to Jinx's, Turbo immediately knew I was not him."

"What did he do?"

"He fluffed himself all over like a toilet brush and hissed at me. He spat, making the fire-engine noises cats do when they are angry, and he lunged at me to claw my eyes out. Jinx's trainer thought Turbo had lost his mind."

"What did you do?"

"I told him to shut up. 'I am Jinx's brother. He is all right; he will come back tomorrow,' I said, but Turbo was too mad to listen. Or maybe because he was deaf. He drove me nuts. The only reason I let him live is that I had promised Jinx I would not hurt his cat, no matter what. So, I bit my tongue but never touched the darn thing."

"And then?"

"The humans locked him away for the night. The following day at training, Jinx and I switched back. I surely hope he gave Turbo a good talking to when he went home. I, for one, was glad to be back in a catless home. Bad enough, they had kids, *quoi*? I do not understand why people do not just keep fish. Or even better, plants."

Guinness and I laughed, but Viper wasn't kidding. He couldn't understand why anyone would bother to take care of useless creatures that don't pull their weight. Viper is the kind of guy who'll die working and feel sorry for every day off he ever took.

Guinness shook her head.

"Malligator Newsflash: There are things beyond work, Viper.

Like love and friendship and fun. Someday you may find out. So, where's Jinx now?"

Viper looked away.

"He is gone."

"Gone where?"

"He died."

I gasped.

"Oh, Viper, I'm so sorry! What happened to him? Did he hit an IED?"

"No. Jinx was too good for that. They put him down."

"They put him down? Why?" Guinness asked.

"One day, when they were on a mission to apprehend a suspect, Jinx attacked his trainer. He bit him, over and over, and would not let go until his handler shot him. His handler wounded him so badly that they had to put him down."

Guinness and I stared at each other. What do you say to your friend whose twin brother got shot by his own handler?

We smelled the sorrow and the anger in his heart, and we felt them too. People call that empathy, but we call it friendship. I licked his nose. Guinness followed.

Viper sighed.

"Sometimes, I wonder if it was him or me who died."

Viper's raw pain burned our souls.

"But...but why?" Guinness asked.

"That is what I always wondered. Why did Jinx attack his trainer? And if he did, why did he not kill him? I plan to find out someday."

The menace in his voice made us shudder. I still do, even though it was like a lifetime ago.

But I remembered what putting down means. Putting down means killing.

Brown is planning to kill me.

28

If I hadn't heard it with my own ears, I couldn't believe that my own human, the person I loved all my life, wants me dead. I had a hard time wrapping my head around that. Maybe he was kidding, I thought. But, as time went by and I stayed in jail, it became evident that Brown wasn't kidding.

Thank Dog for Diane. No matter how stressed out and tired she smells, she still pets me, takes me out, and never fails to slip me a taste of whatever deliciousness she has concocted in the kitchen. Diane is my only hope. Sooner or later, she'll talk Brown into his senses, I thought.

Until the day Diane didn't come home.

She took me out in the morning, gave me a taste of the green beans casserole with French onions she had in the oven, and then left to get the kids from school. I waited and waited for them to return. Dinnertime came and went, dusk became dark, and I was still alone. I crossed my legs, waiting for someone to bring me some water, or at least let me out, but nobody came.

The sun was up by the time Brown came home. He clipped on my leash but not my pizza cutter, and he loaded me in the car where Lovely was waiting.

I feel naked without PC. Especially with Lovely staring at me while pretending she isn't. It's bad enough to lose a leg, but lose your prosthesis too? That's negligence.

Nobody says anything, but the tension is so thick you could chew on it like a marrow bone.

I decide to act cool. I turn my back to Lovely and stare out the window like I'm busy driving. I'm worried about Diane, and I'm burning to ask about her, but I don't want to give Brown the satisfaction of ignoring me. I try to think about something else. Like, where are we going?

And it just dawns on me. Diane's gone, so Brown decided to put me down.

I stare at the trees rushing by, sporting a shy shade of green, and I wonder what being put down feels like. And what will happen next? Will I join Nora? Who will look after Diane and taste her food? Who'll ever teach Aleta how to grow a tail? Who'll help BB out of his meltdowns? Will Tariq ever try his prosthesis and walk again? Will Guinness and Viper miss me?

Oh, boy, how I miss them.

My heart heavy, I lay my nose on my paw and close my eyes.

"Hey, Butter?"

I open one eye. Lovely cocks her caramel-colored head and stares at me, her ears hanging low. She looks guilty and stinks of remorse.

"I'm so sorry."

That does it. If I wasn't sure before, now I know. I'm history.

I close my eyes.

"No, really. I'm sorry."

"What for?"

"For being snarky to you the other night. And for all your troubles. You know, Butter, I never meant to take your place. But I didn't have a choice, you know. When Brown got me and told me about you, I couldn't wait to meet you. I knew you're a hero and all that. I looked up to you and couldn't wait to learn from you. I have no idea how things went so wrong."

I can smell that's true. And Lovely really didn't do anything wrong. I did. I hated her because she was whole and young and pretty, and I treated her like crap.

"I don't know either. You'd think one paw out of four shouldn't be a big deal. After all, I had three left, plus the pizza cutter. But it looks like it was."

"Oh, Butter, how I wish we had this conversation weeks ago."

"Me too. But what can you do? It's too late now."

"You really think he'll put you down?"

I glance at Brown's strained dark face in the mirror. His knuckles are white as he clutches the wheel.

"Yep."

"Can I come with you?"

I eyeball her to see if she's kidding. Common, sister. You brought me here, and now you want to come with me? Really?

"I don't think Brown will let you. You're his partner, after all."

Lovely opens her mouth to say something, but the car pulls into a driveway and stops. Brown gets out and clips my leash. We're facing a long building smelling like dogs and cats. That must be where they put them down.

I tumble out of the car and waltz away on my three paws.

"Good luck, Butter."

"Thanks. Hey, Lovely. Can you do me one last favor?"

"Yep?"

"Tell Diane I love her and the kids. And tell her I know BB will be OK."

You wouldn't think Lovely's ears could get any lower, but they do. She looks like she's crying, even though we all know that dogs don't cry.

But then, she's not the one about to die.

29

Brown drags me inside before I can answer. I check the execution place: gray concrete floors and drab tan walls smelling of disinfectant and grief. The blonde girl at the desk doesn't look like a killer, but then how would I know? I haven't met many killers. She smiles at me as she takes the leash from Brown.

"Thank you for taking her on such short notice. My wife got in a car accident last night. She's in the hospital, and there's no one to look after the dog."

Diane? In the hospital? How about the kids? My heart skips a beat.

"I'm sorry to hear that. I hope your wife does alright."

"Me too."

Brown leans over to pat my head.

"Bye, Butter. Be a good girl."

Seriously?

The girl leads me down a dark corridor that stinks like disinfectant. I follow her into a vast room packed with kennels holding every possible kind of dog. I step in, and they all bark like the mailman is coming.

I'm in shock. Seriously? Are the humans really going to kill all of them? But why?

The girl puts me in the only empty cell and gives me food and water. It looks like it will be a long wait.

The inmate to my left, a Great Dane, sniffs my way.

"Who are you?"

"I'm Butter. You?"

"I'm Thor. How long are you here for?"

"I dunno. As long as it takes them to get to me, I guess. You?"

"Until tomorrow. My family had to go to a wedding, and I couldn't fit in the car."

My jaw drops. They'll put you down for that? I thought I had it bad, but at least I bit Brown. This horse of a dog will die just because he couldn't fit in the car? That's ridiculous!

The scrawny mutt across from me stares at me like he knows me from somewhere. I sniff him. Nope. Never met him before. I know it since I never forget someone's smell. But he won't quit staring.

"What's up, dude? Who are you, and what's your problem?"

He wags his itty-bitty tail and dances on his paws.

"I'm Charlie. My folks dropped me here to go visit a relative."

Now that's downright weird. Putting down your dog for a social commitment? That makes my respect for the human race plummet. And I thought Brown was bad.

"Eh, ma'am?"

"Yes, Charlie?"

"You said your name was Butter?"

"Yep."

"Would you happen to know a K-9 named Guinness?"

I jump to my feet.

"Guinness? A black German Shepherd with brown eyebrows, a wicked sense of humor, and a lousy attitude?"

"Yes, ma'am."

"Where is she?"

"I don't know, ma'am, but I met her a few months ago at the veterinary hospital."

"Guinness? Really? What was she doing there? Was she sick?"

"She got shot, ma'am, but she was on the mend."

"Wow! Did she go back to Afghanistan?"

"I don't know, ma'am, but I don't think so. So you are that Butter? Corporal K-9 hero Butter?"

I'd blush if I knew how. But I don't, and that's good since Charlie is on a roll.

"Corporal Guinness told me all about you. She told me how you found all those bombs, saved hundreds of lives, and then got shot on a mission. She told me about your medal too. She's terribly proud of you, ma'am."

"Call me Butter," I mumble. I'm choked with a smorgasbord of emotions: longing, pride, and love for my friend Guinness. Her old words to some random mutt came back to remind me that I'm actually worth something. I'm not a useless three-pawed; I'm a freaking damn decorated hero.

Charlie clearly agrees.

"I wouldn't dare, Corporal Butter. I'm so honored to meet you. Thank you for your service and for your sacrifice."

I struggle to find words, but I don't need to. The whole kennel erupts into barking, so they couldn't hear me anyhow.

"Thank you for your service and for your sacrifice, Corporal Butter."

30

And just like that, I'm the star of the kennel. From the Saint Bernard to the Pekingese, they all want to know about Kandahar and about my service.

"What is it like up there?" Thor asks.

"Hot and dry. More dust than around a cement factory. And I never found a single place to swim."

"Do they have snow?"

"Not where I was at. I heard they have snow up North, in the mountains, but I never saw it. And there's like no rain."

"No rain? So there's no mud?" Charlie asks.

The kennel gasps. If there's one thing we, dogs, all agree upon, it's mud. Mud is comforting, healing, and delightful. Mud soothes your toes, cools your skin, and makes you smell sexy. That's why we all love mud baths. Sadly, few humans know that, so they avoid it like we avoid shampoo.

"No mud. But there are no baths either. Water is too precious to waste on a K-9 who'll get just as dirty in an hour."

"Have you met the local dogs?"

"I saw a few. Those dogs are not like us. Other than the Afghan hounds, they don't have breeds like we have here. They're all scrawny and so hungry, they'd eat anything, even their own humans.

From Thor to Charlie, they all stare at me like I've lost it. But that's true. Dogs there are more like hyenas. You wouldn't want to meet them on your own. They hunt in packs, and Dog bless you if they happen to meet you before dinner. That happened to Viper once, and he barely lived to tell the tale.

I was on my first deployment when Viper caught a whiff of a hot, willing local lady of the night. She was off base somewhere, but Viper being Viper, he managed to escape outside the wire to look for the love of his life, and he found her. Unfortunately, she was surrounded by a pack of local dogs competing for her favors who decided to have Viper for dinner.

"They came at me like ten on one," Viper said, licking a fresh wound on his leg. "They ambushed me, and I had to run away."

I stare at him, and I can't believe it.

"You? Ran away? That can't be."

Viper flattens his ears.

"Yep. I've never done it before, but there was no other way to get out of there alive."

"How did you get back inside the wire?"

Viper looks away.

"I have my ways."

"Didn't they follow you?"

"Sure they did. But after I killed the first two, the others had enough to eat."

That's not the kind of story I should share with these folks here. It's so ugly that I can barely believe it, even though I know Viper never lies. So I figure I'll change the subject.

"You guys wanna learn how to sniff for IEDs?"

They howl with excitement, so I teach them how to sniff for IEDs and sit next to them rather than dig them out, and they all start practicing in their cells.

Sometime that night, it dawns on me that I'm not here to die. They can't really put down all these dogs, even though some of them smell bad enough to deserve it. Brown brought me here to stay while Diane isn't home.

What happened to her, I wonder? And the kids? I wish there were someone I could ask, but there isn't. So, to distract myself, I chat with Charlie and ask him about Guinness.

"When did you last see her?"

"In the fall, Corporal Butter. She left the hospital the day before I did."

It's spring now, so it's been a while.

"How did she get shot?"

"She didn't say. She seldom spoke about herself. She mostly spoke about you. That must be because of her work for the CIA."

The CIA? Guinness never worked for the CIA! She trained in the North Country and came to Kandahar as a rookie! That's got to be another one of her tricks. What was that girl up to?

"What did she tell you about the CIA?"

"Nothing, really. But there was this one-eared orange cat who taunted me all the time. He told me that I was useless and ugly, and no one would ever want me. He harped on and on until Corporal

Guinness got mad, even though she didn't know me. She raised her heckles, stared the orange in the eye, and growled:

"Shut up, Van Gogh, you useless feline, if you don't want me to tell everyone what you did. You and I both know it. You'll be the laughingstock of the kennel."

"How do you know my name?" the cat hissed.

"I know everything. I work for the CIA," Corporal Guinness said, and the cat went silent.

"Did he leave you alone?"

"Of course. Immediately."

Yep. That's my girl Guinness, bluffing her way out of disasters, as usual. What a dog!

"Corporal Butter?"

"Yes."

"Would you please tell me about Corporal Guinness? I admire her greatly."

So I did. I told Charlie about the day we met when Guinness peed out of her crate on a golf bag smelling like cats. I told him how she found her first IED, how she chased her tail in her crate out of boredom, and how she was the best friend I ever had.

"There's something about Guinness. She's sparky, she's funny, and she can be a pain in the butt. But whenever she's around, you know you'll never be alone."

I choke and look away.

"You miss her," Thor said.

I nod, and I lay my nose on my paw, wishing I could sniff Guinness's butt and lick her nose one more time. But it wasn't meant to be. There's no way I can get back to Kandahar.

The little mutt smells my thoughts.

"I don't think Corporal Guinness went back to war. I think she went into civilian life. She left the hospital with a man she called Pig. You may be able to find her."

"I wish."

"Me too. I'll be glad to help spread the word. How can Corporal Guinness find you?"

How can she find me? I don't know. Who knows where I'll be next?

Then it dawns on me.

"Tell her to look for a one-legged kid named Tariq."

31

Days came and went, and dogs came and left while I stayed put.

So much so that I started wondering if Brown's new plan was to let me rot here instead of ever taking me home. Better than putting me down, I guess.

But little Charlie's words had rekindled my spark. After I got shot, I got so caught up in self-pity for losing my paw, my job, my family, and with it, my whole reason for being that I forgot who I was.

My heart broke when Brown got Lovely and rejected me. And for a good reason, but I forgot that Brown doesn't owe me any more than I owe him. He brought me up and trained me, but I saved his life over and over.

Yes, he needed to get another dog to go back to the freaking war, but he didn't need to be a jerk about it. He could include me and ask me to help train Lovely instead of ignoring me and making me feel useless. But he didn't. He rejected me, and I got so upset that I forgot that I'm no longer Brown's dog.

I'm Bionic Butter, a freaking decorated K-9 hero. I won't let myself go to pieces just because Brown says I'm useless. Thanks to

Charlie and Guinness's praise from afar, I remembered that I deserve better.

So, when the girl at the desk brought a visitor, I wasn't desperate to see them. I was curious, of course. I hoped it was Diane, but I couldn't care less if it were Brown riding Lovely.

It wasn't Brown, and it wasn't Diane. It was a small woman dressed in black who looked familiar, but I couldn't put my paw on where I met her until I sniffed cardamom on her clothes.

"Hi, Butter. I'm Tariq's mom."

Of course. Tariq. The kid with one leg and a tablet.

"I came to invite you to stay with us."

That's weird. Nobody ever invites me anywhere. They either take me somewhere, or they don't. But invite me?

"I spoke to Mr. Brown, and he said it was fine with him if you wanted to stay with us for a while."

That's humbug. Brown said no such thing. He said something like, "Go ahead and take her if you want; just make sure you watch your kid. She's a killer."

"Really. How kind of Mr. Brown."

The woman has the grace to blush.

"I believe that Tariq has a lot he can learn from you. He has no friends, you know. He refuses to go anywhere or meet anyone. He spends all his time on his tablet, and he is so lonely. In the beginning, I was glad that it took his mind away from his pain, but now I worry that it is no longer helping him. My son needs to accept his condition before he can move on. I hope you can help."

Really.

"What exactly would you want me to do?"

She shrugs.

"I am not sure. Just be there and spend time with Tariq, I guess? Your grace and poise in using your prosthesis would go a long way in having him try his before he outgrows it."

I'm not sure what grace and poise are; they must have something to do with PC. But I don't even have my pizza cutter. Brown dropped me off without it, so all I can do is waltz.

The woman clears her throat.

"I must also mention that before I talked to Mr. Brown, I took the liberty to contact Ms. Diane and ask for her advice."

"Really? What did Diane say?"

"Ms. Diane informed me that you retired from active duty due to your disability and that you are interested in employment opportunities. She suggested that I offer you a job. So, I came to enlist your help in mobilizing my son. Ms. Diane said that you are not interested in money. We do not have much money anyhow. But she mentioned that you are a discriminating gourmet with a taste for exotic cuisine, so I brought a few samples of my cooking for you to test."

She takes out a few plastic containers and places them in front of me.

The scents of allspice, nutmeg, and cumin fill my nose and make me drool. I haven't had anything but kibble in ages, but right here, there's creamy white labneh with za'atar, juicy lamb kebab, green shiny dolmas wrapped in grape leaves, and fragrant biryani chock-full of carrots and nuts.

I drool so hard it hurts as I devour one dish after the other. This is better than any Middle-Eastern food I've seen on this side of the Tigris. Even better than Diane's.

When the food's gone, I stop to breathe. There are a few crumbs on the floor, so I clean them too, then look at the woman with new respect.

"Wow! That's incredible. Where did you learn to cook like this?"

"At home, in Iraq. My son and I are refugees. We came to the US after Tariq's father, who worked as a translator for the US Army, got killed in a suicide bomb attack."

32

That's so sad. I'll never forget Abdul, our Afghan translator. He was a lovely man who hoped to make Afghanistan a better place for his daughters. He used to bring us home-cooked meals to make us feel welcome. We loved him.

The Taliban didn't. If there's anyone the Taliban hates more than us, K-9s, it's the Afghan translators. They call them traitors and attack them, their homes, and their families to discourage anyone who'd want to help us. Even I, a bomb-sniffing dog, can't think of a more dangerous job than being a war translator.

Tariq's father must have been a brave man. What a terrible loss for Tariq and his mom! They had to leave their home to immigrate; then Tariq got cancer and had his leg cut off. Compared to theirs, my problems feel small.

There's no freaking way I could say no to helping them, even if this woman cooked like a donkey. But her food is so good that it makes me feel guilty. I almost wish that it were lousy, so I could feel virtuous. But not quite.

"I accept your job offer. When should I start?"

Her face lights up like a Christmas tree.

"As soon as it is convenient. Maybe…"

"Today?"

"Yes, please. Let me work through the details."

She gathers the empty dishes and she's about to leave when I realize that I don't even know her name. To me, she's Tariq's mom. But that's not right. She deserves to be her own person.

"What's your name, ma'am?"

She beams.

"I am Amira."

I wag my tail.

"Glad to meet you, Amira. I'm Butter."

She laughs.

"I know."

Minutes later, she's back with a leash.

"Mr. Brown said he will drop off your prosthesis. Can you walk at all without it?"

"Of course."

I waltz out of the kennel, and we drive to Tariq's house.

"Hey, Tariq. You have a visitor," Amira says.

Tariq watches me waltz in, and his eyebrows join in worry.

"What happened to you?"

"Nothing. Anything happened to you?"

"Where's your prosthesis?"

"It should be coming any moment. How about you? Any news?"

He shakes his head and goes back to his game.

I hope I didn't come all this way for nothing.

Amira leaves us, and I lie by the bed, thinking. I'm out of death row, I'm out of the kennel, and I even landed a job paid in good food. Advantage me.

But to keep my job, I'll have to get this kid moving, and I have no freaking clue how to do it.

I panic. My skin tingles and my heart starts racing. What on earth am I doing here? I'm about to go back to feeling crippled and useless, when I remember Charlie's words. I'm a darn war hero, while Tariq is just a sick child with too much on his plate. He's had enough to deal with. Time to relieve him of his responsibilities. That's what I'm here for.

"Tariq?"

"What?"

"Tomorrow, we're going for a walk."

He stares at me.

"What?"

"I'm here to get you moving, and I plan to do exactly that. Tomorrow we're going for a walk."

He laughs.

"I don't think so, Buster."

"I'm not Buster. I'm Butter. Corporal K-9 Butter, Purple Heart decorated hero to be precise. And I'm telling you that tomorrow we're going for a walk. Get ready."

He's not sure how to take this, so he just looks away and mumbles:

"Get lost."

That night I stole his tablet.

33

Now let me be clear. You may think that we, K-9s, are subordinate to our human handlers. Not exactly. While we obey their orders, we OUTRANK OUR HANDLERS. I didn't mean to scream here, but I think it's essential. When Guinness came for her first deployment, she was as green as a K-9 gets, but she still got promoted over her handler's grade. Why, you ask?

Some say it's to prevent our handlers from abusing us since that would mean assaulting a superior. But that's poppycock. We're in better shape than they are, we're better trained, and we have better teeth. Even now, on my three paws, I could take down Brown before he could say Marrow Bone. Unless he used his gun.

I think the reason we outrank them is to remind us, K-9s, that we aren't there to blindly obey orders. We must use our judgment and ignore any order that could get our handlers in trouble, whether they like it or not.

That's why I felt no shame stealing Tariq's tablet. I'm not here to listen to his orders. I'm here to get him moving, and I get paid for it in delicious food better than what I got in any of my deployments. I have a job, and I'm going to do it whether Tariq likes it or not. I just hope the pizza cutter arrives in time, but if it doesn't, I'm going to waltz my way alongside him.

That morning, Tariq wakes up and reaches for his tablet. It's not there, of course, and he can't believe it. He looks under his blanket, under his pillow, under his bed. Nothing.

Then he looks at me.

"Where's my tablet?"

"How would I know?" I ask, munching on a hot, crunchy falafel just off the fire.

He stares at me.

"Are you lying to me?"

"I never lie. In fact, most dogs never do." I move on to my hummus. It's creamy, salty, garlicky, and just downright delicious.

"Did you take it?"

"Yes."

His eyes would wilt you if you were that kind of person. But I no longer am.

"Give it back."

"After our walk."

"I'm not walking anywhere."

I move on to my tabouleh. I know it's not really a K-9 thing, but I love parsley. Especially in chicken piccata, even though it gets stuck between your teeth. It has this freshness...

"Give me my tablet."

"Of course. After our walk."

"You damn dog!" He jumps out of his bed and falls on his face. Because, unlike me, he hasn't practiced.

"Mom. MOM!"

I start on my dessert. It's fudgy daheen sweetened with date syrup, crunchy with dried coconut, and loaded with enough clarified butter to give you a heart attack.

Amira rushes in.

"What happened?"

"That damn dog stole my tablet. Give it to me."

Amira stares at me. I stare back, and she looks away.

"Sorry. I do not know where it is."

"Well, look for it, damn it!"

Amira is about to kneel and look under the bed when I growl.

"You hired me to do a job. I'm doing it. Don't get in my way."

She clears her voice.

"I am sorry, Tariq. I cannot help you. Butter is in charge. She will get it for you when she thinks you are ready."

"Butter? A dog? You let a dog be in charge?"

"Better than a silly kid," I say, and Amira makes herself scarce.

Tariq crawls back to his bed. He's so angry that his ears are fire-engine red. They look good on him, I think. I lay my nose on my paw and catch a nap.

The shadows have grown short by the time I wake up. I need to go out, so Amira brings my leash and fastens my pizza cutter, and I can smell her worry.

"Tariq is not happy."

"Of course not. If he were happy, he wouldn't do a darn thing. He's got to get unhappy enough to get moving."

Amira nods. "You are right. Is the food OK?"

"Excellent. Keep it going."

The evening goes pretty much the same: Tariq stares at the ceiling; I lie with my nose on my paw, thinking about my people.

The sun is down when he asks, "When are you going to give me my darn tablet?"

"After we go for a walk."

"I don't want to go for a walk."

I ignore him to inhale my masgouf. It's crispy golden carp skewered and grilled. I wasn't much into fish—I thought of it as cat food —but this dish changed my mind.

Tariq balks.

"That's not dog food."

"I know. I'm not a dog. I'm Butter, a decorated K-9 officer. I don't do dog food."

He looks like he'd like to kill me. I wag my tail.

"I understand. But to kill me, you'll have to catch me first. And that means walking."

I slept like a baby that night. Not because I enjoyed frustrating him—I really didn't. But because I felt that I finally had a job and a purpose. I'll get this kid walking if I die trying. It felt good to be in charge again.

When he woke up the following day, Tariq looked for his tablet, then glared at me.

"How long, the walk?"

34

The walk wasn't long, but getting ready took forever. Adjusting Tariq's prosthesis was harder than fixing mine. His fake leg was not a plastic pizza cutter like mine. It was like a real leg, with knee and all, made of shiny metal with a plastic foot at the end.

Amira stuffed Tariq's stump inside the artificial leg, put a sneaker on his plastic foot, and got him his crutches.

Tariq's mouth tightened into a narrow line as he struggled to stand, looking anywhere but at me. I didn't mind. I knew where he came from. He felt comfortable lying in his bed playing on his tablet the whole day. Learning to walk again wasn't much fun, and he resented having to do it.

Even worse, he loathed being told what to do. Throughout his illness, he got used to telling his mother what to do, and she did it. But that didn't work with me.

We filed out of the house, PC and I first, then Tariq, then Amira, ready to help him. That reminded me of my Kandahar missions when I was the first to walk outside the wire. I looked for explosives while everyone else stayed safely behind. But this wasn't Kandahar, and there were no IEDs. The only thing ready to blow up was Tariq's temper. And boy, did he have a short fuse!

Between balancing on his crutches and moving his metal leg, Tariq's every step was a challenge. His face got strained and his knuckles went white around his crutches as he wobbled, struggling to keep his balance. Right behind him, her eyes dark with worry, Amira stood ready to catch him.

Between his anger and her worry, I was exhausted by the time we reached the gate. As we started along the sidewalk, a cool breeze smelling like spring hit my nose, but nobody else seemed to notice. Tariq's whole energy was focused on hobbling down the sidewalk, and Amira only had eyes for her son.

I stopped when we reached the first corner.

"That's good enough for today, don't you think?"

Tariq glared at me and turned the corner. I followed him, filing that for later. Rather than listen to me, he'll do the opposite even if it hurts. So that's the way I'll have to play it.

He turned the next corner, then the next. By the time he hobbled back inside and plopped on his bed, I felt like we'd been gone for a week.

"My tablet?"

I pointed my nose to his side table, where I'd dropped his tablet as we left.

He no longer looked at me that day.

35

Tariq hid his tablet under his pillow that night. What an amateur! You have a lot to learn, my friend, if you want to outsmart an old bomb-sniffer whose job is to find things that don't want to be found.

I stole it, hid it, and got ready for a fight.

"Damn you!"

His eyes pierced me with impotent anger.

"You stole it again!"

"Of course. What did you expect?"

He punched his pillow, then clutched it and hid under his cover to cry.

I felt bad. The last thing I want to do is to add to Tariq's burden, but I can't let him sit and rot in that bed. He has to get up and live, and that requires a good kick in the butt. But he's entitled to his privacy and dignity, whatever is left of them, so I lay my nose on my paw, pretending to sleep, until he calls his mom.

"Let's go. Bring me that stupid prosthesis."

We file out again.

"We don't have to go as far as we did yesterday if you're feeling tired," I say innocently. "That was too much for you."

I watch him push himself even further. He's getting good at it, too. He gets steadier with every step, and he's no longer exhausted by the time we get back.

Just as we reach the gate, it starts snowing. Fluffy snowflakes twirl in the air like feathers, then settle on the ground, the trees, and the tired little house, covering everything with a dazzling white blanket. I open my mouth and stick my tongue out to catch them, but they vanish before I get to taste them.

Tariq lifts his face to the sky and closes his eyes. The soft flakes melt as they touch his burning cheeks, leaving behind clear water drops and, for a moment, he seems to smile.

Back in his room, he glances at his tablet.

"Where did you hide it?"

I wag my tail.

"You're funny."

He shakes his head and goes back to his tablet, but seconds later he puts it down.

"Are you going to do that every day?"

"Yes."

"Until when?"

"Until you're ready to be on your own."

"I'm ready."

"I don't think so."

"What do you want me to do?"

"You need to do the right thing without being forced to, just because it's the right thing. You owe your mom to get better. You owe it to yourself. And we both know you won't get any better by lying in that bed."

His hands clench into fists.

"Do you realize what it feels like to lose a leg?"

"As a matter of fact, I do."

He glances at the pizza cutter and blushes. He was so incensed he forgot all about it. He sighs and goes back to his tablet.

The following day, he doesn't even look for his tablet. He gets up, we get ready, and we file out.

But today, we're in wonderland. Yesterday's snow has covered the drab world in brilliant white. The trees, the mailboxes, the roofs, even the ugly concrete sidewalks—they all sparkle.

"This is so beautiful. In my country, we seldom get snow," Amira says.

Tariq shrugs.

"It's cold," he says, but his eyes sparkle.

The snow doesn't help with the walking, but it's good for the soul. We do our tour and, as we get back to the gate, Tariq starts over. Amira's eyes shine with tears.

"Thanks, Butter," she whispers.

"Don't mention it."

We get back, and Tariq glances at the tablet for a moment, then looks at me.

"You don't have to hide it anymore."

"Good," I say. But I'm going to hide it anyhow.

"What's next?"

"Next?"

"Yes. How much further do I have to walk?"

"I don't know. It's not just the walking. It's about getting your life back. Doing things. Meeting people. Whatever matters to you. There's more to one's life than a leg."

"How did you get to be so wise, Butter?"

"By being stupid."

Tariq's face lights up as he laughs, and he's suddenly back to what he should have been all along: a happy kid.

36

We settled into a routine. We took longer and longer walks every day. Before long, Tariq ditched a crutch, then the other; he used a cane until he learned to walk on his own.

He wore long pants, of course, and boots, so nobody could tell he had a fake leg, unlike me, with my bright blue pizza wheel that drew every eye. People often asked about it, especially the kids, and Tariq couldn't wait to answer.

"She's a war hero. She lost her leg in Afghanistan, and then she learned to use a prosthesis."

"Wow! What courage! What determination!" people said, and Tariq beamed with pride. I wondered how much of it was for me and how much for himself.

Life was pretty good until Tariq got invited to an old friend's birthday party.

"I'm not going."

"Why not? We will buy her a nice gift and...."

"I'M NOT GOING."

He turned around and slammed the door. That was one problem with getting him walking: He could walk out on you whenever he felt like it.

"He's going. Just buy that gift."
I followed him. He glared at me.
"I'm not going, no matter what you say."
"Why not?"
"They all know I've lost my leg. They'll stare at me and maybe even ask about it."
"So?"
"I don't like that."
"Why?"
"I'm uncomfortable."
"Tariq, you have to be uncomfortable to grow. You were uncomfortable walking, and you were uncomfortable leaving the house not long ago. And look at you now!"
"I'm not going!"
We went.

I don't think they expected him. Faces grew long as he walked in the room, steady but flushed with emotion. Tentative smiles and awkward greetings followed. It would have been a total cluster, but for my pizza cutter. PC was the life of the party.

The kids' faces lit up when they saw me, and they gathered around me, bombarding Tariq with questions.

"What's her name?" our host, a cute redhead, asked.
"She's Corporal K-9 Butter."
"What happened to her leg?"
"She got shot in Afghanistan."
"Can she do any tricks?" a chunky little kid asked.
Tariq's face darkened.
"She's not that kind of dog. But yes, she can detect bombs."
Eyes widened as everyone looked at me with new respect.
"Where did you get her?" a sour-faced teenager asked.
"As a matter of fact, she got me. She came to help with my recuperation."
"Isn't that cool."

I wondered if he was so sour because Tariq stole his show. Before we arrived, Sour-face must have been the life of the party.

"I wish I had a cool dog like that," Chunky said. "Mine has four legs, not something cool like this."

Tariq laughed, and the others did too. I ate too much cake, and I had so many hands petting me that I almost longed for a bath. But Tariq was happy, and that was all that mattered.

They saw us to the door when Amira came to take us home.

"Hey, Tariq," Sour-face called.

"Yes."

"I'm having a few friends over for pizza and a movie on Friday. Wanna come? With Butter, of course."

"Sure."

I went to bed feeling accomplished. My work here was done. From now on it's just the fun.

37

I knew something was up as soon as I heard the doorbell. We, dogs, smell these things. It's like the universe sends us messages. The doorbell sounded the same, but I just knew it wasn't the mailman.

I was right. I was chatting with Tariq in his room when I heard Diane's voice. I ran out to meet her, but I stopped dead in my tracks when I saw her leaning on a cane.

"Diane! You're back! How I missed you! How are you?"

She laughed and cried and hugged me.

"I'm good."

"The kids?"

"They're fine too. How are you?"

I wagged my tail.

"Great. Even better now that you're here."

Amira offered her a seat, then coffee, and we sat looking at each other in silence. I don't know why, but the air suddenly got so thick with tension you could chew on it.

Amira cleared her voice.

"What happened to you, Diane?"

"I got in a car accident. I broke my leg, and I had surgery. But I'm much better now that I ditched my crutches."

"How are the kids?"

"They're great. They keep asking about Butter."

About me? I don't know. They didn't seem to care much when I was in jail. But I let that pass.

"How are you guys doing?" Diane asks. "How is Tariq?"

"He is doing great. Butter did a fantastic job. She got him walking. He got so good on his prosthesis that he no longer needs a cane. She also helped him reconnect with his old friends, so he is no longer lonely. Our Butter is a miracle worker."

"She totally is. We miss her terribly at home."

Who's "we"? I wonder.

"Aleta keeps asking: 'When is Butter coming home? I miss her!'"

The room's so quiet you could hear a fly sneeze. Amira pours some red juice into glasses and the noise breaks the silence like a hammer.

"This is homemade pomegranate juice. It helps with healing," Amira says.

Diane takes a sip and sets the glass down.

"It's delicious. Thank you."

We sit staring at each other, pretending there's no elephant in the room.

Amira clears her throat.

"Tariq is very fond of Butter. He looks up to her in every way. She is the only person he obeys. I am so glad that she is here to set him straight."

Diane nods.

"I can see that. Butter is amazing. I knew that from the day Joe brought her home. She was so tiny she fit in the palm of my hand, and I had to wake up every night to feed her milk from a syringe. Butter is my first baby, before Aleta and BB, and I couldn't love her more. To me, Butter is not a dog. She's family. We all miss her terribly."

Amira takes a tiny sip of juice.

"A bit tart, no? Please correct me if I am wrong, but Butter seemed to have some rough times in your home. She did not get the love and respect she deserves. Here, we cherish her. Nothing is too good for our Butter."

Diane's mouth tightens.

"Every family has problems and needs time to work them out. Things change. New situations and new family members may throw things out of whack for a while, but one must work on them and find a new balance."

Amira's smile doesn't reach her eyes.

"Of course. Situations change. People do too. I know I did. I must make a confession: In my culture, people do not think much about dogs. They see them as dirty animals. Where I come from, being called a dog is an insult. I am sorry, Butter, but I have to be honest with you."

She clears her throat.

"I had a hard time asking for Butter's help. I only did it because I was desperate. My son Tariq had a hard life, harder than any child should. He was only eight when his father died, leaving him to be the man of the house. That was already too much responsibility for him. Then we came to the US. He left behind his home, his friends, and everything he knew. He had to learn a new language and adjust to a new culture. Then he got cancer and went through countless painful procedures. With his leg, he lost his hope and his desire to live. I watched him get deeper and deeper into depression, and there was nothing I could do to help him. When his doctor told us about Butter, I had no choice but to give it a try. She was my last resort."

Amira's voice breaks.

"We were fortunate that Butter agreed to help us. Please forgive me, Diane, but she would not have come to us if she got the respect she deserved in your home, and you know it."

Diane nods, her eyes cast down.

"This hero dog came to my son's rescue. She put up with his disrespect and his ugly moods. She somehow managed to get him out of his shell and got him to enjoy life again. Nobody, ever, in my life, did more for me. I worship the ground Butter steps on, and our home is her home, now and forever."

Diane opens her mouth to say something as the door slams open, and Tariq barges in.

"What's going on?"

His mother smiles.

"My friend Diane and I are chatting."

"About what?"

"About Butter. Diane wants to take her home."

Tariq's face falls.

"What?"

Amira shrugs.

"You tell him, Diane."

"Tariq, I'm so glad to see the progress you've made. I'm very proud of you. I'm sure you're very fond of Butter, and I'm glad she helped you through your journey, but now that you've gone so far, her place is at home with us. The kids miss her, and so do I."

Tariq stares at Diane, trying to understand.

"You want to take my Butter?"

Diane's eyes move from his troubled face to his prosthesis. She clears her throat.

"I'd like to take Butter home."

"But this is her home. We love her here."

"I can see that. Butter is a lucky girl to have you and your mom care so much about her. I'm glad to see her happy and content."

She leans on her cane to stand up.

"I have to go now. I'll tell the kids that Butter is doing great. I'll be back."

She hugs me and slips me a strip of smoky homemade beef jerky.

"I'll be back soon."

I feel guilty as I watch her hobble out, leaning on her cane.

She's my mom, and she's always been there for me when I was in trouble. And she needs me.

Tariq leans over me, wobbling on the prosthesis he poorly adjusted himself.

"Butter?"

"Yes?"

"I love you."

38

That night, I lay awake watching Tariq's steady breathing as he slept, and wondered what to do.

    I'll have to choose between going back home and staying here to help Tariq become the man he needs to grow into. I know what life with Tariq would be like. But home? I don't know. More of the same? Brown, flaunting Lovely in my face to make me feel old and useless? Diane, sneaking me snacks and trying to protect me from his wrath? The kids, who don't know what it's all about, torn between the old doggie and the pretty doggie? I don't know.

What would Guinness do?

I remember the night when Guinness, Viper, and I lay in our crates talking about the meaning of life.

It had been a bad day. That morning, Carlos one of our soldiers, just twenty-three, shot himself in the head before dawn. That was the beginning of our saddest day in camp.

We woke up thinking we were under attack. The men jumped out of their cots, grabbed their kits, and ran into position. They looked long and hard for the intruders, but there was nothing. It took us a while to find Carlos lying on the dusty ground behind the trucks. That was the only place he'd found some privacy. The men tried to revive him, but it was too late. The thirsty Afghan desert had sucked his blood and his life.

It was a terrible time for all of us. The patrol was canceled, and the men spent the day talking about Carlos, trying to understand what happened. All but Carlos' best friend, Leo. His face ashen, his shoulders slumped, Leo sat staring into space smelling like guilt. The lieutenant tried to give us a pep talk, but he had no pep left either.

"What the heck is this all about, *hein?*" Viper asked, his long black snout up in the air like this whole grizzly affair was beneath him.

Guinness shrugged.

"I guess he didn't want to live any more."

"But why?"

Guinness cocked her head to stare at him.

"How about turning this question on its head. What was he living for?"

"Are you serious? He had a job to do!" Viper spat.

"Viper, did it ever occur to you that not everyone lives for their job?"

Viper stared at her like she'd gone nuts.

"What else is there?"

"Lots of things. Friendship, love, and justice, and food, and the good of the planet, and the polar bears, and...."

"Have you lost your mind? The polar bears? Who cares about the polar bears?"

"I do. I once saw a documentary showing how baby polar bears starve to death because of climate change. Their moms can't find food anymore, and...."

Viper shook his head with impatience.

"Common, Guinness. Carlos did not kill himself for the polar bears."

"Probably not. But my point is that there are things in life even more important than doing a job."

"You're wrong. There's nothing more important, I assure you."

"Maybe not to you. But others may think otherwise. Butter?"

"What?"

"What's the most important thing in life for you?"

I hate to be put on the spot between these two. They could argue day and night and then forever, but there I was.

"I don't know. A few things. Friendship? Love? Loyalty? Feeling that you make a difference in people's lives?"

Guinness wags her tail in agreement.

"Atta girl, Butter. There, Viper. I rest my case. There's more to life than work."

Viper glares at her and opens his muzzle to say something nasty when Sabrina, his handler, comes and hugs him.

Viper's ears go down, and his tail hides between his legs. He's mortified. Viper hates hugs, and he'd love to get away, but he doesn't want to hurt Sabrina's feelings, so he sits there as she sobs, hanging onto his neck. He tries to ignore her until he can't take it anymore.

"There, there. Everything will be alright. Just wait and see. It's going to be OK."

He licks her tears, and she finally relents.

"Thank you, Viper. This is so terrible! Poor Carlos couldn't take it anymore. You know, I could never do this without you. Your love and support make all the difference in the world. I'm so happy I have you."

Guinness and I exchange glances but say nothing. Like really, what is there to say? Viper sees us and seethes.

"That was nothing."

"Of course."

"She just needed some moral support. She was upset that her buddy died."

We cock our heads. Viper growls.

"OK, OK, go ahead and tell me. What's the most important thing in life? What do we live for?"

"Love? Friendship? Feeling like our lives weren't wasted?" Guinness says.

I can't disagree.

"I think we live to make a difference. We want to leave behind something good that wouldn't have been there if it wasn't for us. Whatever that is."

"I get you. We live to make a difference on earth. To leave the world better than we found it. That's a tall order."

That was the one, and only, time I heard Viper admit that he was wrong.

Now, as I watch Tariq sleep, I wonder what to do. How can I leave the world better than I found it? I fought in Afghanistan for most of my life. Day after day, I put my life in danger, choking on the dust, suffering through the heat, and living on MREs. That war took my youth, my leg, and my friends, and I don't know that I made any difference.

And I was young and whole. Now, that I'm old and crippled, and running out of time, can I still make a difference?

Or is it too late?

39

Day after day, I struggled to figure out what I should do to make my life matter and I got nowhere.

Tariq needs me. He's not ready to be left by himself. He's about to start school, and he'll need a kick in the butt and a shoulder to cry on when things don't go his way.

Diane needs me too. I've never seen her so exhausted. No wonder. She's got to hobble on that cane and look after Aleta, BB, and the house by herself. And she's got no one to listen to her worries, taste her food, supervise her cooking, and lick her nose to make her feel better.

The day Diane returns, still leaning on her cane, I still don't know what to do.

Amira pulls her a chair and pours her sweet mint tea. They sit, and we stare at each other.

Diane clears her throat.

"What a nice day."

I glance outside. It's only noon, but it looks like dusk. A howling wind whips the rain into the windows as the sky grows darker by the minute.

"Very nice," Amira says.

I cock my head, staring from one to the other, trying to figure out if they lost their minds or if they're speaking in code, but they go quiet.

That's when I figure it out. It's just "throat-clearing"—the human equivalent of sniffing each other's butt to establish common ground before getting to the real deal.

"How have you been?" Amira asks.

"Much better, thanks. I should ditch the cane in a few days."

So maybe Diane doesn't need me anymore. I don't know if that makes me happy or sad.

"How about you guys? What's new with you?"

"We are doing good. Tariq looks forward to starting school next week. He can hardly wait to be with his friends every day."

There now. It looks like Tariq doesn't need me either. My ears drop. A few days ago, I was so hot they fought over me. Now I'm last week's news.

"How are the kids?"

"Great. Growing like weeds and asking about Butter all the time."

So, do they still want me? I want to ask, but I don't want to sound needy.

Diane sets down her tea.

"Listen, Amira, what will you do with all your extra time when Tariq goes back to school?"

Amira shrugs.

"I have not thought about that. I will get a job, maybe? We could surely use the money."

"I have an idea," Diane says.

"Yes?"

"Tariq's doctor asked me if I could take Butter to visit other kids who lost their limbs, like Tariq did. Most of them have trouble adjusting to living without a limb and struggle with their body image. That makes it hard for them to reclaim their lives. She thinks that Butter may help those kids like she helped Tariq."

"I see."

"But, as you know, I have my work and the kids. I don't have much spare time. I thought maybe we could share the work? You know so much more about this than I do. You could tell them about Tariq and maybe even show them pictures. That may help."

Amira cocks her head in question like I've never seen a human do.

"Diane, are you saying we should share Butter?"

"Pretty much. I'm saying let's help Butter do what she does best: Help people. To feel accomplished, she needs to have a purpose and feel useful. She could help those children who struggle like Tariq did."

Amira sighs.

"What do you think, Butter?"

What do I think? I'm not sure what I think, but feeling useful is what I need. If I could help those kids like I helped Tariq, I might still make the world a better place.

"I'd love to be useful. I live for that. But where are these kids? And what do I do with them?"

Diane smiles.

"Some are in the hospital, waiting for their surgery or recovering from it. Some are at home, learning how to walk and struggling to reclaim their lives. You'd visit them, like we did with Tariq, and help them see that losing a leg is not the end of the world."

"And I'd sometimes go with you, and sometimes with Amira?"

"Yes. Maybe even with Tariq, if he's willing."

"Where would I live?"

"Where would you like to live, Butter?"

"I want to go home."

40

But that's a lie. I don't want to go home. I have to go home.

Not because of Diane, as much as I love her. Not even because of the kids. Because of Brown.

I can't let Brown have the last word. He abandoned me, shunned me, locked me in my crate, then ditched me in that kennel and left me there. I can't let that pass. I couldn't respect myself if I did.

I won't bite him again, no matter what. I no longer am the

bewildered, insecure Butter that he used to bully. I'm Corporal Butter, a Purple Heart–decorated K-9 hero and a working support dog. I'm not ashamed of my missing leg; I'm proud of my pizza cutter and everything I've accomplished with it. I'm proud of who I am.

That's what I tell myself as Diane drives me home, and I pump myself up to meet Brown and Lovely. I just wish I could believe it.

I felt so lost that I couldn't figure out what to do. So I wondered: What would Guinness do?

And I know she'd do precisely what I'm doing. I can almost hear her: "Butter, you can't let the bastages get you down. Go and show them who's boss."

But I'm not Guinness. And, to be honest, I don't so feel good about this.

I'm worried about what's coming. I'm concerned about Brown and Lovely. I'm also worried about Tariq and Amira, and I feel guilty about leaving them.

When I left, Tariq was so angry he didn't even say goodbye. He went back to his bed and his tablet and didn't even glance at me when I said goodbye.

Amira sobbed. "That's terrible! What will I do if he goes back to where he was before you came, and you're not here to deal with him?"

I licked her hand. It tasted like butter and honey. And tears.

That made me realize that if there's only one person—one person here that I should help, that's Amira. Not because of her fabulous cooking. Not even because she pried me out of the kennel that Brown left me in. But because Amira has the most growing to do. Not Tariq. He'll figure it out eventually. Not even Diane. She'll ditch her cane and go back to being her competent self. The most challenging path is Amira's. That girl needs to grow into her potential, and I know she can, but she doesn't.

I lick her tears, and she doesn't pull away. It's been a while since she avoided touching me. But we've never been this close.

"Amira, you'll do exactly what I did. You'll take away his tablet, and you won't give it back until he does what he needs to do."

"But he'll ask for it!"

"Of course he will. And you'll say no."

Amira shrivels, and I choke with guilt. But she needs to grow like Tariq did.

"Amira, Tariq is not the man of the house. He's just a little kid who needs help, boundaries, and guidance. You are his mom. You have to guide him whether he likes it or not. You can't let a kid take control of your lives. That's unfair to you both. It's your job to make decisions."

Amira sighs.

"I guess you're right, but I just wasn't brought up that way."

"But you can learn. If you love Tariq, you have to set him straight. And I'll be back, remember?"

She hugs me and gives me a brown bag smelling like cardamom and roses.

"There's a little something I made for you with love. Enjoy!"

"Thank you, Amira. I will."

The scents from the brown bag make me slobber as I sit in Diane's car, watching the roads I know so well. But I can't touch food now. My stomach is in turmoil, and my heart is too. I'm afraid to go home. I'm terrified to see Brown, and I dread seeing Lovely, but I have to. So I keep telling myself:

"Don't let the bastages get you down. Go show them who's boss."

41

The car turns right, and I recognize every mailbox, every yard, and every bush, even though they're now all dressed in green. The old lady's calico cat sits in her usual window, cleaning her paws. She pretends she doesn't see me, but I know better. She's still mad at me for chasing her so far up a tree they had to bring a ladder to get her down. But Wiry, the terrier across the street, sees me and yaps like crazy.

"Butter! You're back! Good to see you, partner! I missed you!"

I wag my tail to say hi, but I'm busy. My heart pounds as the car stops in the driveway, and Diane lets me out. I sniff the mailbox and check-in as the door opens, and the kids run out screaming.

"Butter! Butter! You're back."

Aleta hugs me. She got so big that she's taller than me. I lick her face, and she laughs.

"Doggy! Doggy!"

BB is next. His black curls tickle my nose, and I sneeze. They all laugh but Diane. She wipes her tears as I lick the chocolate off BB's face.

"Butter? Butter?! Butter!!!"

Lovely explodes through the door barking like crazy. She runs so fast that her caramel-colored ears float behind her. She salutes with a downward dog, then turns around to offer me her butt to sniff. I oblige. She's had chicken kibble for breakfast, she's healthy, and she's totally thrilled to see me.

I turn around to let her sniff my butt. She does it respectfully, then comes around and licks my nose. My heart melts. Nobody's licked my nose since Guinness, and that's the most fantastic feeling in the world. Try it sometime. It will give you warm fuzzies.

I lick her nose, and we start jumping and playing like puppies. The humans laugh, even Brown. He stands in the doorway, looking smaller than I remembered.

"Butter?"

I stare at him.

"How are you, Butter?"

I wag my tail.

"Fine, thanks. You?"

"Come!"

He slaps his hip.

I sit.

"I don't think so. I'm fine right here, thanks."

His face darkens.

"I said..."

Diane interrupts, "You said you were sorry, didn't you, Joe? You said you were sorry you were mean to Butter. You said you wish you didn't humiliate her and mistreat her, didn't you, Joe?"

"But..."

"No, but. That's what you told me only last night. Otherwise, I wouldn't have brought Butter back. You said you were stupid and mean, and you promised to make it up to her. Remember?"

Diane's gaze pierces Brown, and he sighs.

"Yes."

"So?"

He takes a deep breath like he's about to jump in cold water.

"I'm sorry, Butter. I'm sorry for being harsh to you. I wish I was smarter and kinder. But I was scared, you see. When you got shot, I was devastated. I tried my best to keep you alive. But when it became obvious that you couldn't go back to work, I still had to. That's my job and our livelihood, so I had to take another partner. That's why I got Lovely. I didn't really have a choice."

He sighs.

"But Diane is right. I should have treated you better. But I was a coward. I couldn't bring myself to come back and tell you that I got another dog. It was easier to just leave you there until Diane brought you home. And then I felt even more guilty.

"When I brought Lovely home, that made it worse. I felt embarrassed and guilty, even though it wasn't really my fault. I should have tried to include you, but it was easier to feel angry than guilty. So I shut you out and ignored you. You responded with anger, so I felt justified to shut you out even more. I'm sorry."

I smell that's true. Brown was too weak to support me and too weak to admit to his guilt.

"I understand."

He smiles and opens his arms.

I stay put.

"I don't think so, my friend. I know all about unconditional love. I tried it, and we both know how that worked for me. If you want love, you'll have to earn it."

I walk inside with Lovely, and the kids follow. Diane brings in the brown bag.

"This yours, Butter?"

"Oh, yeah."

My heavenly smelling cardamom cookies. BB and Aleta grab them and start chewing. Lovely looks at them and drools.

"Help yourself."

"What are these?" Diane asks.

"Hadji Badah, Amira's unique Iraqi cookies. That girl could teach you a thing or two about Middle-Eastern cuisine, you know."

Diane gives me a side glance.

"Just check them out."

The cookie crunches as Diane bites into it.

"They are good! I'll have to ask her for the recipe."

I wag my tail.

"Are you kidding? Ask me! Flour, eggs, cardamom, rose water, sugar, almonds...."

42

Being back has been bittersweet. Everything is the same and still so different. The kids are still a lovely full-time job. Diane ditched her cane and got back to work, and she's glad I'm back to help with her cooking. Our latest creation, Grandma's Spitting Cake, was a hit. My idea, of course.

"Come on, Butter! That's silly. I can't put the whole plums in!"

"Why not?"

"What if someone bites into them and breaks a tooth?"

"Like really? How come they don't break their teeth while eating plums?"

"But they know the stones are there!"

"So, tell them. It's a swell idea. You get to have a spitting contest with dessert. Whoever spits further gets to win. It's more fun than watching TV."

Diane shrugs.

"I don't know, Butter. If I keep the plums whole, the batter will rise better, but who'd want to do a spitting contest over dinner?"

"Come on, give it a try."

"If you insist. But I still think it's a bad idea. And you don't even know how to spit."

"Says who?"

Diane proceeds to wash and dry the plums. She flavors the batter with lemon peel and cinnamon, pours it over the plums, and sighs.

"I don't know, Butter...."

"How bad can it be? There's always ice cream."

"Yeah. But I hoped to do better for their last supper...."

Brown and Lovely are heading to Afghanistan tomorrow. This is Lovely's first deployment, so I did my best to teach her everything I know. I hope they send them to our old base in Kandahar to work with Viper and Guinness. I know Charlie said Guinness retired, but you never know.

I did my best to prepare Lovely.

"You can always trust Guinness. Always. Whether you like what she tells you or not, she's probably right. She always is."

"How about Viper?"

"He's usually right too, but he's got this snotty Malinois attitude that makes it hard to listen to him. But you can trust him with your life. He's the kind of guy who'll tell you if you have parsley in your teeth, though you won't find much parsley there. They're more into MREs. Regardless, never fail to ask for advice. Nobody will laugh at you. And if they do, so what? That might just keep you alive."

Lovely licks my nose, and I lick hers. I'm terribly worried. I wish I could be there to help her.

"Thanks, Butter. Thank you for your friendship, and your teaching, and all the kindness I know I don't deserve. Is there anything..."

"Dinner, everyone," Diane calls.

We gather into the dining room for supper. The kids are in their high chairs; I sit next to Diane, and Lovely sits next to Brown, as usual, but it's been a long time since I seethed with hate. Now Lovely is my friend, and I'll miss her terribly.

The bacon-wrapped sweet potatoes with spicy chili dip are perfect. The bacon's crispy, the potatoes smooth and sweet, and the chili dip gives them that extra kick that makes your mouth water.

Even the kids, who'd rather eat their boogers than people's food, polish them off.

Juicy meatloaf with mashed potatoes and horseradish sauce comes next. The horseradish makes you cry in a good way. I sniff my way through it, hoping it won't settle on my hips.

And now to the pièce de résistance! Our cake is golden, fragrant, and smothered in whipped cream. Diane should be proud, but it's Grandma's Spitting Cake, and she's anxious.

"Today's dessert is presented by Butter, who wanted to make dessert into a game. The plums have stones, so please be careful. Once you find a stone, you're ready to play."

The house smells like sweet vanilla, tangy plums, and lemon zest, and I choke on my drool. Brown smiles.

"You outdid yourself, Diane." He takes a bite, and he puckers.

"I got a stone. What do I do?"

"Spit it as far as you can."

Brown spits, and the stone hits the ground two feet from his toes. Not looking like a winner.

"Maybe next time."

I work my way through the cake and save my two stones.

"My turn!"

Aleta spits her stone beyond Brown's.

"Like really?" he huffs.

"Me too! Me too!"

BB doesn't talk much, and he seldom engages with others. He inhabits a world of his own, spinning the wheels of his truck or staring at lights. But this silly game drew him in. He spits his stone, but not far enough, and he sits back looking forlorn. He's got no stones left.

I lick his hand. He opens it, and I drop a stone in his hand.

Aleta's next try is better than her last. Diane drops her stone on her best skirt. Brown makes no progress. But BB does better, and he claps his hands.

"I have one left," Diane says and proceeds to drop it between her toes.

BB stands up, holding my last stone.

"Me. Me."

He puts the stone in his mouth and spits it. It hits the side of the table and ricochets, falling far away. BB straightens up, smiles, and looks at his mom.

"I won."

Diane hugs him with tears in her eyes.

"You sure did, sweetheart."

I've never seen her so proud.

The following morning is our last. The kids say goodbye to Brown, then hug Lovely as I watch from the kitchen. Brown comes to say goodbye.

"Goodbye, Butter. I'll give your regards to your friends."

"Thanks. But more importantly, look after Lovely. She needs all the help she can get."

He frowns.

"You think I need reminding?"

I stare at him until he lowers his eyes, then I wag my tail and go say goodbye to Lovely.

"Be careful, Lovely, and you'll be all right."

"Thanks, Butter."

"Tell Guinness I love her, but don't say that to Viper. He doesn't do love. Just tell him I'd be glad to eat his mutton anytime."

My throat tightens as I watch them file out the door. I wonder if I'll ever see them again. War is a harsh place to be, and tomorrow is not guaranteed. But I know that Lovely will do her best. She's a bright girl with an excellent nose. And Brown will look after her and teach her like he taught me.

I'll keep my toes crossed for them.

But in the meantime, I need to get ready. I have a big day today. Amira and I are visiting a one-legged kid named Peter.

ABOUT THE AUTHOR

Rada Jones was born in Transylvania, ten miles from Dracula's Castle. Growing up with vampires taught her that humans can be fickle, but you can always trust dogs and books. That's why she read every book she could get, including the phone book (too many characters, too little action), and adopted every stray she met, from dogs to frogs.

After joining her American husband, she spent years studying medicine and working in the ER, but she still speaks like Dracula's cousin.

Rada, her husband Steve, and their dog Guinness live in a cozy Adirondack cabin supervised by a deaf cat named Paxil. They spend their days writing and hiking.

To sign for updates, freebies, and to get in touch, check out Rada-Jones.com.

AFTERWORD

Thanks for reading Bionic Butter. I hope you enjoyed it. If you did, please spend a minute to leave a review and tell a friend. You may help others find this book.

Becoming K-9, Book #1 in the K-9 Heroes series is available now. K-9 Viper, Book #3, is now on preorder.

Visit RadaJones.com to sign up for updates, get freebies and stay in touch. I love hearing from you!

Rada

EXCERPT FROM BECOMING K-9
A BOMB DOG'S MEMOIR

Who knew training humans was so hard? You'd wonder why. They aren't that stupid. It takes them a while, but they eventually learn when you want out, you're hungry or you're thirsty. They can even talk to each other by making noise with their tongue. How weird is that? Even my brother Blue, who's the slowest of us all, knows that the tongue is for lapping water and panting to cool down.

Mom cocked her head and licked my nose.

"That's the best they can do, dear. They have no tails, their ears don't move, and most don't even have enough fur to raise their hackles. No wonder they're confused and need us to guide them. And that's what we do; that's our life's work. But we need to choose them carefully."

Mom was on her sixth litter and very wise. Beautiful, too, with her long muzzle, amber eyes, and smooth, shiny fur, all black but for her golden legs and loving pink tongue.

She glanced at Yellow, who chased his tail instead of paying attention, and growled. He hung his head and sat in line with the rest of us to listen.

It was a lovely summer day as Mom homeschooled us in Jones's front yard. The warm wind tickled my nose. I bit it, but I caught nothing. I tried again, but Mother threw me a side glance, so I closed my mouth and sat still.

"Boys and girls, today's the day. People will come to check you out and choose which one to take home. They don't know it, but it doesn't work that way. You choose your humans, but choose them wisely. Sniff them all, then pick the ones that smell like food if you want a good life. You may sometimes get bacon, maybe even grapes. Humans say dogs don't eat grapes, but that's poppycock. They just want to keep them for themselves. My grandma was a pure-bred Alsatian, and she loved Riesling. I never had Riesling, but Concord isn't bad."

A shiny strip of drool dripped from Mom's mouth. She licked it off and inspected us. We were seven: three boys and four girls. But that doesn't much matter when you're just ten weeks old. The only difference is how you pee. The boys don't know how to squat so they need something to lift their leg to, like a bush or a mailbox. How stupid!

"Why don't you just lift your leg, if that's what you need to do? What does the bush have to do with anything?"

Mom bristled.

"Leave them alone, Red."

I tried, but it was hard. I was the runt of the litter, so I had to prove myself all the time. Mom said I had a Napoleonic complex.

"What's that?"

"It's when you're the smallest, so you have to be meaner to show them that size doesn't matter."

I told you Mom is brilliant. She came all the way from Germany when she was just a pup. Our human, Jones, has two passions: German shepherds and history. Mom was his first German shepherd, and he spent lots of time teaching her things most dogs never heard about.

He still does, even now that she's old. He sits in his recliner and reads to her as she lays by the fireplace. Sometimes I listen in. There was a story about a dude named Hitler. Not a nice guy, but for loving German shepherds. Another one about that short guy Napoleon who tried to conquer the world while wearing funny hats. And one about some place called Afghanistan.

"That's a bad war, Maddie," Jones said, scratching the four white hairs in his beard. "Those Taliban, they are not nice people."

He calls her Maddie, but her real name is Madeline Rose Kahn Van Jones. He is Jones. The Van is for Van Gogh, some orange dude who got so mad he bit off his own ear. The rest is just for show, since people pay more for dogs with long names; they call that a pedigree. Mom's pedigree is longer than her tail.

As always, Mom was right. People came to see us, and they brought their spouses, their kids, and even their dogs to check us out and choose which one to get. Like, really? Jones said that only one out of twenty German shepherd owners is smarter than his dog. I don't believe it. I bet he fudged the numbers to feel better. You think you own a dog? Who feeds who? Who cleans after who? Who does the work, everything but making decisions? You, human, in case you didn't know it. You don't buy a dog; you hire supervision. But I digress.

My littermates and I wore colored collars so humans could tell us apart. There was no need, really, since we were all different, but humans couldn't see it. What color did I wear? Red, of course. I was small, but I was the queen of the litter, whether the others liked it or not.

A fat man in a Hawaiian shirt stopped to stare at me. He called his female.

"Look at this red one! Isn't he cute?"

She hobbled closer, leaning on her crooked stick. I love sticks, so I tried to take it. She didn't want to let go, but I insisted. They laughed.

"Let's get him."

Jones cleared his throat.

"Red is lovely, indeed, but she's a very active little person who needs a lot of attention. How much time do you plan to work with her every day?"

"Work with her?"

"Yes. Walk her, train her, and play with her."

They stared at him like he'd lost his marbles. He smiled.

"May I recommend Brown here? He's lovely, easygoing, and eager to please. He'll be happy to lay on the sofa watching TV. Or Miss Green? She's a polite little lady who gets along with everyone and never disappoints."

Brown left. So did Green, Yellow, and even White, while I stayed, waiting for my forever home.

"Take it easy, Red dear," Mother said when there were only two of us left—Black and me. "You need to soften up a bit; otherwise, you'll be left without a family. People look for easygoing dogs to fit into their lives, not for somebody to take charge. Though maybe they should, really, but they aren't smart enough to know that."

Her German accent made her words feel harsh. Have you ever listened to Germans? It's like they're constipated while they also have a cold. They keep clearing their throats, so their words come out like bullets from a machine gun. I don't speak German, but I love watching old war movies with Jones.

"What do you mean, Mom? What should I do?"

"Lick their hands, sweetheart. Wrap yourself around their feet and stare at them like they hung the moon."

"Are you serious?"

"Of course."

"But they're stupid!"

"Come on, Red, don't be so judgmental. You're just a pup, and you have so much to learn. A nice family will give you a good life. They'll love you, play with you, and spoil you. Knowing you have a good, safe home will lift a weight off my soul."

You think I listened? You've got to be kidding. That's how I ended up in the military.

<u>BECOMING K-9:</u> A Bomb Dog's Memoir
(K-9 Heroes Book 1)
ASIN: B08XKBGXN3

EXCERPT FROM VIPER
THE VETERAN'S STORY

The day they shot Butter I lost a piece of my soul.

We, dogs, can often smell things before they even happen, but I didn't see that coming. The day started like every other day in Kandahar. Butter, Guinness and I woke up at our base to the smell of fake mutton the handlers mixed in our kibble. That got Butter drooling, as usual. That Lab's always crazy about food. She thinks of herself as a discerning gourmet, but I doubt it. No foodie would eat the MREs for pleasure. I only eat it enough to keep up with my nutrient uptake, but I hate it. I wish Sabrina would stop doctoring it with these fake aromas. If it's good for me, it's good for me – I'll eat it just like I'd eat any disgusting protein shake. But I don't tell her, since I don't want to hurt her feelings. The poor girl thinks she's a chef, but I bet you she couldn't cook anything if it didn't come out of an MRE bag.

But it's not her fault, of course. She's fresh out of training, and she does her best to deal with the heat, the insurgents, and the men. She's got nobody else but me to look after her, so I do my best to protect her but I pretend I don't care, since I don't want to ruin my Malinois reputation. They all think I'm a jerk who only cares about his job, and that's just what I want. I'd rather look like a neurotic curmudgeon than a softie.

I watch Butter inhale her food like it it's a Sundae. The old girl is getting chubby. She looks great in her shiny golden coat, but that extra weight is no good for her joints. In our line of business, the lighter, the better, but Butter doesn't think about the future. She's into here and now, and she's always hungry, like most pups who never had a loving mother. That's why I give her my food. And because it keeps me slim.

I expected we'll stay inside the wire today. Since the insurgents went crazy, we've been on patrol every day, and our humans look worse for the wear. My girl Sabrina could do with some sleep. So could Brown, Butter's handler. The only one who's found her groove is Silver, Guinness' handler. After Bear, her first K-9, blew himself up just to prove a point, Silver has had some rough times until she came back with Guinness, but since then, they've been on a roll.

Oops. I forgot to mention Guinness. My bad. But I thought you already knew. Hard to believe there's anyone who doesn't know Guinness. For a three-year-old K-9, she makes quite a splash. Sure she's pretty, with her sleek black coat and her funny brown eyebrows making her always look surprised, but that's not it. Despite being a German Shepherd, Guinness is a rebel with a lousy attitude, a wicked sense of humor, and a complete disregard for authority. That girl is just wired differently: she comes up with things that nobody thought about, and does stuff nobody else dares. She's a firecracker, and I sure wish she wasn't neutered. That's all I'll say about that.

But rest was not on the agenda. After breakfast, Sabrina got me kitted for patrol in my bulletproof vest and we filed behind Butter and Guinness towards the Green Gate. Butter is in the lead, Guinness in the rear, and I got the spot in the middle that I hate. That has me inhaling everyone's dust and following others' decisions. But it's my turn.

The Green Gate creaks open, and Butter steps outside the wire, dragging Brown on his 30 feet leash. She stops and we wait. And waited.

I don't know what she's doing – thinking about some pizza recipe, admiring the dusty landscape, or maybe she fell asleep – but she keeps us standing there under the brutal Afghan sun until I can not take it anymore.

"No rush, Butter, *chérie*. Take your time. After all, we have nothing better to do today. And the landscape is charming."

Guinness growls.

"Shut up, Viper. She knows what she does better than you do."

That, I can not argue with. Whether she's composing a haiku or deciding what leash to wear for her next date, she knows what she's doing and I don't. And I'm OK with that. What I'm not OK with is standing here with my tongue hanging down to my knees, waiting for the action to start.

She finally gets moving. We file behind her towards the village to look for explosives, since the insurgents have gone crazy planting IEDs. They've got to have hidden the stuff somewhere, and there aren't many places in this God-forsaken desert.

But we didn't find anything in the village. Nothing but mud houses with curtains instead of doors, water jugs and occasional chests, and people glaring at us. That's the one thing I can't get used to after years of military life. I got used to taking orders from humans who don't know half of what I do, breathing the damn dust, and melting in the heat. But I can't get used to the endless hate.

We file behind Butter and head back to our camp. My throat is parched and my tongue skirts the ground as we drag ourselves back. I can't wait to be back inside the wire, drink cold water and lie in the shade, but Butter takes her sweet time, sniffing every speckle of dust like it's new, even though we were here just an hour ago. Then she stops, and I can't take it.

"Take your time, Butter. After all, you wouldn't want to ruin your hair, *hein*?"

She wags her tail and cocks her golden head. She opens her mouth to tell me where to put it, but gunshots blast and Butter tumbles to the ground in a cloud of dust.

<u>**K-9 VIPER**</u>: The Veteran's Story
(K-9 Heroes Book 3)
ASIN: B095N21LSD

CPSIA information can be obtained
at www.ICGtesting.com
Printed in the USA
LVHW081550200223
739935LV00029B/468